FAMILY TIES

Blood vs. Water

By

Cornelia Smith

Cornelia Smith

Copyright © 2015 by Cornelia Smith

All Rights Reserved

Published by Cornelia Smith

Edited by

1st Edition

This is a work of fiction. Names, characters, places, and incidents are a product of the author's imagination. Locales and public names are sometimes used for atmospheric purposes. Any resemblance to actual people, living or dead, or to businesses, companies, events, institutions, or locales is completely coincidental.

This book or any portion thereof may not be reproduced or used in any manner whatsoever, without the express written permission of the publisher, except for the use of brief quotations in a book review.

For permission requests, you may email the author at Cornelia.Smith17@yahoo.com

TABLE OF CONTENTS

PROLOGUE	1
CHAPTER 1	6
CHAPTER 2	12
CHAPTER 3	15
CHAPTER 4	20
CHAPTER 5	26
CHAPTER 6	30
CHAPTER 7	36
CHAPTER 8	44
CHAPTER 9	48
CHAPTER 10	53
CHAPTER 11	60
CHAPTER 12	66
CHAPTER 13	73
CHAPTER 14	76
CHAPTER 15	80
CHAPTER 16	84
CHAPTER 17	90
CHAPTER 18	93
CHAPTER 19	96
CHAPTER 20	101
CHAPTER 21	105
CHAPTER 22	112
CHAPTER 23	116

CHAPTER 24 121
CHAPTER 25 125
CHAPTER 26 131
CHAPTER 27 136
CHAPTER 28 141
CHAPTER 29 144
CHAPTER 30 148
CHAPTER 31 151
CHAPTER 32 155
CHAPTER 33 158

PROLOGUE

Fall 2002

Bam! *Bam! Bam! Bam! Bam! Bam! Bam! Bam!* The house rumbles. The walls shake. It scares seven-year-old Chloe out of her sleep. Cold sweat slides down the side of her cheek. "Momma!" she yells out with static in her voice.

"I'm going to ask you one more time woman. Where the hell were you when I called?" Ray's deep baritone sent chills down Chloe's spine. She knew that tone oh so well. Arguing had become a part of Ray and Cheryl's daily routine.

Chloe glances over at her baby sister Clover; checking to make sure that she was still fast asleep. Fortunately, she is because the dispute only got louder. Chloe wraps herself up in her tiny arms and rocks back and forth; searching for a peaceful rest stop for her mind. The fighting is something she can't get used to. She stares at the colorful picture on the nightstand.

Calling the people in the picture a happy family is an understatement. Life was good for the McCray's, but that all changed once Ray lost everything he valued in one year and turned to alcohol for comfort. First, his mother, then his job, and finally the one thing he prayed so hard for, his son. Cheryl had tried to hold on to their baby as she knew Ray couldn't take another loss, but her stress had picked up after he lost his job, and no matter how hard she tried not to worry, she did. As the bills piled up, so did her stress.

"I told you before, I was here getting your kids ready for school," Cheryl pleaded.

"Bitch you must think I'm some kind of fool." He swallows and straightens his back. His eyes intent, set on Cheryl's beautiful brown eyes.

"Why must we do this every night Ray? I'm tired, I can't do this anymore. I just can't." Tears stream from Cheryl's face.

"Oh, now you want to leave me? This must be that nigga talking. So, you letting that nigga come between your family Cheryl? Is that it?" There were no words in the Webster's Dictionary that would convince Ray that Cheryl wasn't cheating. The alcohol brought out his insecurities, and Cheryl knew there was nothing she could do to dodge the ass whooping that was bound to come, so she figured leaving him wouldn't hurt the situation much.

"That's it, I'm through. I'm taking my kids and we are out!" Her words hit like daggers to his heart.

"Cheryl, don't play with me woman. Don't go messing with my kids." His voice almost breaks as he pleads for Cheryl's cooperation.

"I have had it with you Ray; I'm tired of you taking me and my kids through this shit every night." As soon as Cheryl snatches Chloe up from the crack of her bedroom door, Ray pens her in a choke hold.

"Put her down bitch; now!"

Terrified; Chloe bursts into crying; screaming, "Please stop it you two!"

"Ray, you're scaring our baby," she responds calmly.

"No, you scaring her! All you have to do is leave them out of our shit Cheryl, now put her down!" Ray snatches the cold steel from his waist and rests the hole onto Cheryl's temple.

"Do you think I'm playing with you bitch?" Chloe's crying grows intense; she can't stand to see her father's gun. Him pulling it out is another ritual she hates.

"Are you really going to continue to do this in front of our daughters?" Cheryl drops Chloe to the floor.

"Run into your room and lock the door Chloe!" she blurts out.

"I want to know the truth Cheryl! That's all I'm asking you. You try to make me seem like I'm the crazy one." His bullshit plays on Cheryl's last nerves, so she decides to ride the emotional rollercoaster deep into his insecurities and fear.

"Yes, I'm seeing someone Ray." He gives her hard eye contact. His tone comes back stronger.

"You went out and…. A stranger?" she nods. He groans. He asks again.

"You're cheating on me Cheryl?" Nervously, she nods. Bit by bit, his face changes. Jealousy rises and gives him insane eyes, then he blinks, and looks mortally wounded.

"Look me in my face and tell me you're fucking with me Cheryl?" His eyes plead for her to change her answer. His voice demands her to, but she refuses to let the ride end. In the back of her mind, she hopes the lie will set her free.

"I'm not lying. I've been unhappy for quite some time now, and frankly I feel I deserve better."

The glow of insanity lights Ray's face. Cheryl is more than prepared for round two. She's ready for him to call her names, grab her, hit her, slap her, squeeze her neck, and bang her head against the wall until she loses consciousness. She was used to it. A large part of her wants him to do all those things, so she wouldn't feel bad and chicken out on sending him to jail this time. Another part of her gut was terrified, screaming, "Flee! Don't fight with this dragon!"

The closer Ray gets to Cheryl, the more her body tenses. She eases into sprinter position, but he is closer to the kid's bedroom door. She secretly tries to decide if she should jump off the emotional roller coaster, but before she can Ray pulls the trigger. One blow to the head and Cheryl's body drops to the floor. Shocked at his reflex, he pauses for ten long seconds with his mouth hanging wide open.

"Noooo!" he screams, dropping down to his knees beside her. He had once promised Cheryl he would leave the gun off his waist when he was drinking, but just like the other promises, he broke it. His eyes met with Chloe's as she shivered with fear. A loud, unnerving silence surfaces in the house. Ray tugs at his hair, "Stop looking at me like that for I…"

His anger wanted to play with some haunting threats, but the words won't come. Ray clenches his fist and punches at the air. Veins from his thick neck grow thicker than ropes. He looks as though he wants to take the witness to his crime out.

"Go to your room Chloe!" he yells, but she ignores him. Her body stiffens, feet glued to the floor.

"Don't play with me Chloe, I'm warning you!" Spit flies from his lips, his tone blacker than death. Chloe shivers, but she doesn't move. Low on options, Ray takes the only other option that doesn't require killing his daughter. He flees the scene.

CHAPTER 1

"Nine-one-one, what's your emergency?" For three minutes, Chloe inhales and exhales in short breaths.

"Nine-one-one, what's your emergency?"

"My mother is dead," she responds finally, after gathering up the breath to answer.

"Who am I speaking with?"

"Chloe McCray," she replies softly with static in her voice.

"Chloe how old are you?"

"I'm seven."

"Are there any adults in the house with you Chloe?"

"No, it's just my mommy, my baby sister Clover and me." Chloe's innocence sends a chill up the operator's spine and she responds with a little static.

"What's your address sweetheart, do you know your…?"

"One-three-two-six Hill Street Atlanta Ga, 30315," she replies with the address like a robot. Cheryl made her repeat both her address and phone number until she memorized them.

"Help is on the way; can you tell me what's wrong with mommy?"

"She's dead," Chloe repeats.

"How did mommy die?" Sweat covers Chloe's nose, snot runs down to her lips. Her world was looking hazy, hot and humid. The air was too thick to breath. She swallows, feeling, suffocation; choking on her saliva.

"Take your time."

"She was shot," Chloe softly responds.

"Can you tell me who shot her Chloe? Who shot mommy?"

Bam! Bam! Bam! Bam! Bam! Bam! Bam!

The loud noise rattles Chloe's nerves and she bursts back into whimpering.

"It's okay, it's okay Chloe. That's help at the door." The operator's calming voice did little to Chloe's nerves, her crying just grew more intense. She throws the phone down and curls up in the corner with her face bent into her knees.

"It's Atlanta Police Department, open up the door Chloe!" The whimpering echoed out the door and APD decided not to waste any more time. The door was down on the third blow.

****

"Hey angels," the blonde-haired, blue-eyed nurse approached the girls with colorful blow pops, but Chloe wasn't budging. She hadn't said a word in hours and the police was beginning to think finding Cheryl's killer was going to be harder to do with a witness than without one.

"Do you girls like blow pops?" Nurse Winter asks.

"I do." Without hesitation, Clover took the sucker from the nurse's hand. She was four and very clueless about the activities around her. She slept through the drama and when she finally woke, her big sister's natural instincts protected her from the truth. In fact, Chloe wants to protect her from everybody. Scared of being split apart, Chloe grabs Clover closer to her as if Nurse Winter was the monster from the closest.

"It's okay, she can have the sucker, and you can too." Ray Charles could see Chloe's protective mechanism.

"Would you like a sucker Chloe?" Nurse Winter asks before gently placing the sucker into Chloe's hand.

"Will you play Barbie with me Chloe? I always wanted to play Barbie but I never had anyone to play with." Chloe wasn't buying the sweet talk and distraction. She knew that the nurse wanted something, and she wasn't sure if telling her would help or hurt her situation with Clover. So, her attitude remains stale until Nurse Winter purposely flips over the chairs on her way to the PlayStation in the waiting area. Neither Chloe nor Clover could hold in their laughter.

They laugh hard and fortunately for Nurse Winter; it was the very thing that got Chloe to open up. After hours of playing around and tip-toeing around the big question, Nurse Winter was finally able to get Chloe to tell them who killed her mother. Clover was in the restroom and quietly, Chloe finally broke down.

"I don't want my sister taken from me," Chloe explained to Nurse Winter.

"My mommy would want us together." Pretending to be strong, Nurse Winter pastes a fake smile onto her face.

"Don't you worry about anything; I promise you I'm not going to let them split you girls up." Fear invades Nurse Winter's thoughts as the word *promise* rolls off of her tongue. She wasn't sure how she was going to pull off that magic, but she was determined to make Chloe and Clover's life as simple as possible from here on out.

"Can you not tell Clover about my mommy yet? She will cry all night if you do."

Nurse Winter chuckles at Chloe's mommy mode then replies, "Sure, I think I can manage that."

****

"I got good news, but it comes with a challenging task," Nurse Winter explains to the social worker and head detective.

"And what's that?" Ms. Washington, the Social worker, asks.

"I've gotten Chloe to open up to me about her mother's killer, but she is not willing to talk until she knows that she and her sister will not be split up."

"Let me get this straight, you made a deal with a seven-year-old. Couldn't you just bribe her or something?"

"No I couldn't, and yes I did make a deal with a seven-year-old. She's very smart and well, hell, it is her life we are talking about here."

Detective Brown could hear the frustration in Nurse Winter's tone, so he changed his.

"That's true, so we're dealing with a seven-year-old genius? Ms. Washington, I want you to make magic happen. I need these girls put in a stable and very loving environment. They've been through enough drama for a lifetime." Ms. Winter inhaled deep breaths and exhale short ones. She wasn't up for the challenge. The children weren't babies, and to top it off, they were mixed. It was going to be challenging to get them in one stable home.

She gave Detective Brown a stale look then nodded in agreement.

"Nurse Winter, let me to talk to you for a second." Ms. Washington leads Ms. Winter over to the corner.

"I'm not going to lie to you; it's going to be very challenging to get them a stable home in a short period of time. But if you really care about the kids, I can arrange for them to stay with you for a while. At least until I find them somewhere stable." Nurse Winter knew from Ms. Washington whispering that she wasn't exactly following protocol, but she also knew that kids over two had a hard time finding homes in the system, and that most parents weren't looking to take on two at once.

A large part of her instantly wanted to say yes. She had tried for years to have kids, but after her third miscarriage, she and her husband David gave up. It almost felt like a sign, but Chelsey knew taking home two kids off the streets would cause chaos in her home.

"I need an answer now because when I leave out the hospital, the offer no longer stands," Ms. Washington said, breaking Nurse Winter from her deep daze.

"Okay, I'll do it," she sharply responds without thinking about it another second.

"Great, you can come sign these papers, and I'll let you do the honor of telling the girls. Now, these papers are temporary and I'll have to come out to your house to check out things." Nurse Winter blankly just nods at Ms. Washington's every statement as she secretly thinks about the big decision she just made without her husband's permission.

CHAPTER 2

"**S**urprise!" David peeks his head into the room at the sleeping angels, but he didn't see one thing to be happy about.

"Whose kids do you have Chelsey?"

"They're ours David." Thick green veins pop up on the side of David's temple. Instantly, his pressure is up and his hearing was in and out, it was like grenades had gone off, right there in the walls of his home. He glances over at his wife and instantly he wants to lay his paws on her, but he knew that would only make matters worse. So instead, he storms off into the garage. *Bam! Bam! Bam! Bam! Bam! Bam!* The house rumbles. The walls shake. It scares the breath out of Chelsey. She places her hand over her mouth to silence her cries. It had been years since she'd seen David so angry.

She mumbles, "The kids, oh the kids," before she goes to their room in a hurry. On her way out to the living area, she bumps her knee on the edge of the entertainment center, and then falls. She crawls over the area rug, trying her hardest to get to the kids' room to shut their door.

She leans against the wall, holding her leg, cringing, the pain bringing tears to her eyes. The house continues to rumble and shake. It felt and sounded like a car ramming into the walls over and over again.

Bam! Bam!

The house felt like it was about to cave in, like an earthquake was hitting it but it wasn't an earthquake, it was David's raw rage. David was in the garage, in his slacks and button down, punishing his boxing bag.

Chelsey rubs the pain in her leg until it eases up enough to let her stand. The house continues to quake. She leans against the wall, rubs her temple, wipes her eyes, and takes easy steps into the girls' room. Relieved that girls are fast asleep, she eases back out of the room and down the stairs to the living area. After a good twenty minutes of boxing, David makes his way back to the living area where Chelsey waited nervously.

"How could you do this without my permission Chelsey?" He gives Chelsey a heinous scowl and she gives him a Tina Turner glare, hoping he wouldn't do what he was thinking about.

"It's not final David, they are here temporarily." David blinks; exhales in short puffs. The glow of insanity fades from his eyes, but it resurfaces when Chelsey explains, "It's not final, but I want it to be David. I want kids and I can't waste anymore of my time hoping and praying that I will one day produce them. I know you think it will happen, but when David?" Chelsey's voice cracks.

"I feel like you're trying set me up Chelsey. I'm feeling real trapped right now."

"It's not always about you David. What do you think I'm suppose to do? Go through life without having children?"

"No Chelsey, but you know my situation."

"Yes, and you know my situation."

"Having these girls around is going to set me back and you know it Chelsey. You know I will give you the world, but this is something I'm not sure I can do." Tears drip from Chelsey's eyes.

"All I am asking is for you to give us a chance. Let's try it out before we cancel the idea all together." Chelsey's pleading eyes weaken David's heart.

"You know I'm sick Chelsey."

"But you have been doing so well, and I know you can beat this; I know you can David. You're not that person." Chelsey's strong faith in David made him feel like he could really overcome his obstacles, so finally he agrees.

"We can try it out Chelsey, but if it doesn't work, I'm not sure our marriage will either." David's words haunted Chelsey because she knew he meant every word and life without him was a scary thought. Life without kids was an even scarier thought, so she agreed on the gamble.

"Thank you David." Chelsey plants a wet kiss on David's chocolate cheeks before marching up the stairs to her bedroom.

"I mean what I said Chelsey!" David yells up the stairs.

"I'm sure you do baby, but it's going to work. Just watch!" Chelsey yelled back with fake joy in her spirit.

CHAPTER 3

"You look like shit, Chelsey."

"I know. No sleep."

"It's more than that. Looks like you've been traumatized."

Both Chelsey and her sister Jessica were in the parking lot across the street from Benihana. The kids were a bigger task than Chelsey imagined and she just wanted to be around an adult. After being stuck in traffic for almost thirty minutes, Jessica needed a cigarette.

She smacks the brand new pack of Newports on the ass, then impatiently lights up the cancer stick.

"Sister, I wish you would quit those things already."

"I wish it was that easy Chelsey, trust me. I hate the smell of them." Jessica slid her hands through her red, untanned mane before puffing at the cancer stick again.

"You could if you just tried a little harder." Jessica and Chelsey are almost identical in looks, but their personalities are far from each other.

Jessica speaks her mind when and wherever it's required; what comes up comes out with her. Chelsey is more of a reserved, shy and free spirit.

"Listen woman, I didn't break free from my kids to come here and hear you preach to me." Jessica smashes the rest of the cigarette into the concrete with her funky clog shoes. She was a walking model for the trailer park look from head to toe. Her faded jeans had dirt stains on the knees, her multi-colored t-shirt read WHITE GIRL WITH A BLACK GIRL ASS. Her face even appeared to be dingy, though it was clean as a whistle.

"Why did you pull me out the house in the middle of the week anyway? Don't you have to go to work tomorrow?" The girls swiftly jay walk across the busy street and into the restaurant.

"A party of two," Chelsey informs the waiter.

"Why didn't you tell me we were coming to this bougie ass restaurant Chelsey?"

"It's not a bougie ass restaurant Jessica. It just requires you to wear clothes." Chelsey's black leather pants hug her curves. Her black knee-high boots with the thin-heel and pointed-toe give her flat cushion a little boost in the buttocks and her light-brown cotton blouse squeezes her breasts. Chelsey spends most of her days shopping. David is a professor and Chelsey is a registered nurse. Money is pretty good for them, having and no kids gave them more money to spend on their personal highs; David's was electronics and Chelsey's was clothes.

"If you would have told me to dress up, I would have," Jessica added, pulling out a chair at the table.

"What would you have put on? Your black jeans instead of your light ones?" The two sisters chuckle at Chelsey's joke.

"Hey, I didn't marry the black genius; you did." The girls gave David the nickname "genius" because he was almost never wrong about anything. He was sharp, smooth and very smart.

"Speaking of the black genius, how is he?" Chelsey's wide smile thins out and instantly Jessica can tell something is wrong.

"He's fine," Chelsey answers with a fake smile.

"Don't give me that robotic, pre-recorded ass answer Chelsey. What's really going on?" Chelsey's eyes tilt low and her plastic smile slowly disappears.

"You promise you won't judge me Jessica? I can't take any negativity right now."

"I'm not going to judge you Chelsey," Jessica answered without second thought.

"The reason I look like shit is because David and I…Never mind." Jessica's face lights up like a firecracker, she exhales short puffs of breath. Her patience was wearing thin. She was thirsty for the tea and Chelsey was playing around.

"Girl if you don't stop playing with me you better."

"David and I are adopting kids." Jessica tucks her red hair behind her ear.

"Come again?"

"You heard me clearly the first time Jessica," Chelsey replied with an attitude.

"Where did you get the kids from? What sex are they? When did you two agree on something like this?" Jessica couldn't hold in her questions and she was a minute away from making her earlier promise a lie. She was ready to judge with no apologies.

"The kids came from the hospital. The girls witnessed their mother get killed by their father; well at least the oldest one did."

"Oh, so they are older girls, oh okay. That was a good compromise." Satisfied with Chelsey's answer, Jessica's body relaxes as she slouches back into her chair, staring at the menu.

"No."

"No what Chelsey?"

"No they are not older girls. One is seven and the other is four," Chelsey mumbles.

"You must be out your cotton picking mind, Chelsey! Are you fucking serious with me right now?"

"Hello, ladies. I'm Lee and I will be your waiter today. Can I start you ladies off with something to drink?" Lee couldn't have come at a better time. Chelsey tucks her face into the drink menu.

"Yes, I'll have a Blue Bahama Mama please."

"Okay and you ma'am?" he asks Jessica.

"I'll have the same, thank you." No more than two minutes after Lee was gone from the table, Jessica cranks her rant back up.

"It's like you are trying to feed stake to a dog. I really can't believe you Chelsey. I mean you and your husband were doing so well. How does he feel about this?"

"Initially, he was mad, but he agreed to give it a try. I mean Jessica, these girls had nowhere to go, and if I didn't get them, they were going to split them up. Can you believe that? After all the kids have been through they were going to split them up?" There was nothing Chelsey could say that would make Jessica get on board. Her ears went deaf and she drowns Chelsey explaining out with the soft restaurant soft Jazz.

"Jessica, are you listening to me?"

"No, I'm not Chelsey. I'm trying to listen to the good music and you're blowing it for me right now." Jessica's ice cold response sent chills up Chelsey's spine, and the tears without warning trail slowly down her cheeks.

"You promised you wouldn't judge. How could you be so damn could hearted? I don't understand. You have a family, so you'll never understand how I feel." The crack in Chelsey's voice didn't faze Jessica. She never loosens the frown on her face.

"You know what? Fuck you Jessica! You have a nice day." Jessica watches as Chelsey storms out of the restaurant thinking, *damn she's supposed to pay for this shit.* After drinking both her and Chelsey's drink, Jessica decides to call it a wrap. Besides, she didn't bring enough cash to eat even if she wanted to.

CHAPTER 4

The colorful "welcome home" sign hanging from t banister blended nicely with the Dora the Explorer themed table. The candy table was so inviting the neighborhood children couldn't wait for Chloe and Clover to arrive so they could attack it.

"Welcome home momma's babies!" Chelsey yells proudly with her arms opened wide.

"Come give me a hug." Chloe slowly walks away from Ms. Washington towards Chelsey. The word *momma* sounded weird, and she wasn't sure if she wanted to accept it. Although she and Clover were prepped by Ms. Washington on their way to the Winters' house that the paperwork was final and they were going to be with David and Chelsey permanently now, hearing the word *momma* from Chelsey only made Chloe think about her mother Cheryl.

Distracted by the candy table, clowns and gifts, Clover paid no mind to Chelsey's words. She runs full speed into Chelsey's arms, hugs her and even gives her a kiss on the cheek before diving right into the festivities.

"Oh they are beautiful Chelsey. You and David are so lucky," the neighbor from across the street said.

"I know. It's almost surreal." Chelsey, her neighbors and co-workers drank wine while watching their children indulge in the festivities.

"That one seems a little reserved," the co-worker points out, eyeballing Chloe.

"Yeah, she has to warm-up to a large crowds, but when she does; you can't get her to stop talking." Chelsey lies in an attempt to hide her embarrassment. Chloe had declined her hug and skipped out on her kiss. Though it hurt her feelings, she pasted on a smile and tried to ignore it, hoping that no one noticed Chloe's cold shoulder towards her.

"Yeah, she probably just has to warm up to her environment because I talked to her on the way over and she was thrilled about being here permanently," Ms. Washington adds.

She's probably more thrilled about not being torn away from her only blood relative, Chelsey thought, sipping on the chilled red wine.

"Oh, your sister was able to make it after all." All eyes fixate on Jessica as she makes her way through the crowd of children to the kitchen with the ladies.

"She must not have had time to stop and get the kids," the neighbor adds.

"Probably not, she's probably just leaving work," Chelsey quickly throws in her lie before Jessica reaches the kitchen.

"Hey Jessica."

"Hey ladies, how is everyone?"

Like a choir, the girls nod the heads and sing, "Fine, we've been fine."

"Where are the girls?" the curvy nurse asks even after Chelsey answered the question.

"Oh they're home with their father." Jessica didn't bother elaborating on why they weren't with her; she just jumps right into a different conversation.

"So how are you feeling new mommy?" Chelsey's eyes light up like a Christmas tree. She hadn't spoken with Jessica in weeks, since the big blow out, and she was happy to hear that Jessica was willing to try and support her decision to adopt.

"It's very challenging but rewarding all at the same time." Chelsey's answer couldn't have sounded more rehearsed. Her perky housewife vibe made Jessica question if it's the only reason Chelsey would make such a decision in the first place.

"I'm happy for you sister, I really am. I can't wait for the girls to meet their new cousins. I'm going to throw them a sleepover and we're going to pig out in front the television with our faces beat and our toes and nails painted to perfection." The sound of motherhood did numbers to Chelsey's spirit. She begins to prance around the party like one of the children.

****

Clover's tonsils rattle between pauses; she could barely catch her breath. The loud, obnoxious noise was testing David's nerves, but he tried to keep his patience. Chelsey bounces Clover on her knee, shoving everything she could think of into Clover's mouth to stop the crying but

Clover wasn't budging. She tosses the sipping cup, and then throws the apple. After two licks from the sucker, she tosses it as well.

"Shh, shh, don't cry, don't cry big girl." Chloe and David assist the help clean the party up until David loses his patience.

"Give her to me Chelsey." Gently, David takes Clover from his wife's arms.

"Come on little mama." David tosses Clover over his shoulder and softly rubs her back, bouncing her as he paces around the house. After walking around the house for twenty minutes, Clover was sound the sleep. David so badly wanted to remind Chelsey that these days would come, but he bit back the urge.

"Baby, you're so good with her."

"What are we going to do when she has another spell about wanting her mother Chelsey? It's not going to go away just because we ignore her question. We were lucky today because she was worn out from today's festivities." Chelsey could feel David's energy turning from positive to negative quickly.

"I'm not about to do this with you David. Not tonight," she replies, picking up toys off the oak hardwood floor.

"I leave for New York in the morning. I'm going to rent out a room and leave from there. I need some time alone."

"You can't just run every time something gets hard David." Chelsey couldn't hide the crack in her voice.

"I'm not running woman; I just feel like if I stay, you and me are going to eventually bark into a nasty battle, and I'm trying to avoid arguing my wife. Plus the hotel is closer to the airport. I'll be back on Sunday." Without further explanation, David fetches his pre-packed bag out the bedroom and storms out of the house.

****

Get it together Chelsey Winter, Chelsey thought as she fluffed out her blonde pigtails. Her soul was feeling blue but she tried her best to look nothing less than happy on the outside. David was into role playing and Chelsey was desperate to make her marriage work. There was no reason for her not to be able to balance both a husband and kids. She wipes her tears once more before drawing on her eyeliner. The sound of David's footsteps startle her and quickly she smears on the pink, cotton-candy lip gloss on her lips.

"Chelsey."

"I'll be out in a minute," she responds softly.

"Mr. Winter, can you explain to me why I got a D+ on my paper?" Chelsey waves around the blank paper with the D+ written large in red on the front.

"Well you probably just need to study a little young lady." Unsurprised at Chelsey's efforts, David hesitantly plays along with her game.

"Well studying isn't usually my thing, is there something else I can do to bring up my grade?" Chelsey's Sunday pink panties blocks David's view as she bends down to pick up his shoes.

"Oops, I'm sorry," Chelsey fans her checkerboard, catholic uniform skirt down.

"I told my momma I needed a longer skirt." Chelsey had the right plan for the right man on the wrong day. David just couldn't get into what would have been a beautiful night if he didn't feel used. He knew Chelsey was only role playing because their marriage was on the rocks, not because she wanted to. She hated role playing. That fact along with the others that were running through David's head kept his boy from rising. Chelsey fumbles around with David's dick for a short five minutes before he finally tells her to stop. Nothing she was doing could get him in the mood, and it was starting to become more embarrassing than sexy.

"What's wrong?" she asks. "Aren't you attracted to me anymore?" The crack in her voice was irritably noticeable and David was at his breaking point, so he snapped.

"Don't try to make it seem like I'm not into you Chelsey, don't you dare try and turn this around on me. You know full well you're only role playing because of your guilt." Chelsey's eyes water, but it doesn't stop her from telling David off.

"You know what? I'm starting to believe you are just looking for any reason to bitch David. Marriage is about compromise and that's why I'm role playing because I want to make my freaking husband happy. That's what one does when they care about their partner's well-being and happiness." Stung by the truth and stuck on words, David flops in bed and tucks his head deep under his covers. Following his lead, Chelsey snatches the obnoxious knuckle bows out of her head, toss them onto the floor, and flops into bed.

CHAPTER 5

Y*ou know you want it, quit acting like you don't. I see the way you look at me when passing in the halls.*

The sound of the doctor's voice sends chills up Chelsey's spine and she begins to toss and turn.

Oh your pussy is the tightest, tell me you like it. The worse day of Chelsey's life was playing out like a movie in her dream and she couldn't shake it. *Pow! Quit screaming bitch.*

"No!" Quickly, Chelsey jumps up from the nightmare squeezing her stomach as if she was losing her baby all over again. She searches the covers for blood.

"You were having a nightmare," David says softly, rubbing her back.

"You okay? Try lying on your side this time. Every time you lay on your back, you have a nightmare." Before David and Chelsey could tuck themselves back into the covers, Clover's loud vocal alarm rang. She was like an infant. The house had to constantly tip-toe around when she was sleep.

"Damn!" David murmurs before glancing at the clock on the nightstand. 4:45 a.m. It wasn't long before he had to get up for work.

"I got her, don't worry about. Go back to sleep." Chelsey attempts to fetch David at the door but he waves her off.

"Just try and get some sleep Chelsey." After twenty long minutes, David finally returns back into his room.

"Is she sleeping?" Chelsey whispers.

"Yes, finally," he whispers back before chuckling.

"I thought the whole reason for getting older kids was to avoid getting up at night," Chelsey chimes in on the laugher.

"She has some demanding vocals on her boy, let me tell you." David and Chelsey's eyes meet and they're an inch away from a kiss, but neither of them has the courage to take the needed step.

"I don't even know if I should try and go back to sleep," David breaks the silence and says.

"Me neither. Hey, if I never told you, I think you're an excellence father." Slightly, David's heart caves in.

"I'm trying," he murmurs in her ear caressing her breast with his free hand.

"I want us to work David." Chelsey lowers one of the straps on her sequin gown, licks her index finger, and then rubs it over her hardened nipple. The two's eyes meet again and she decides to try and make a move once more. Chelsey takes her breast in her hand, pushes it up as much as she could, and flickers her tongue over the nipple. She could see the excitement in David's eyes and it motivates her to take it to the next level. So she takes David's right hand and pulls him closer to her.

"Taste it baby." Following directions, David lifts Chelsey's gown over her head, exposing her pierced belly button. He palms her breasts in his hands, takes the round earring onto the tip of his tongue and licks her belly button gently. Her pussy gets wet instantly. All she could do was caress the back of his head. She couldn't believe he wanted it too. It had been years since David even attempted to taste her, and months since they actually sexed. For ten long minutes, David gives Chelsey's kitty tongue. They both moan softly. David is into it but not enough to get hard. He could feel Chelsey body tense up. Ten minutes had turned into twenty quick, and he knew she would soon want the real the deal, so he begins to shove two fingers in her juice box while fumbling one finger into her ass. He was desperate to make cum.

"Baby that feels great," Chelsey moans. "Deeper, deeper," she demands and he obeys; sticking now three fingers deep into her.

"Aww, I love you David." Chelsey's body had been yearning for David's touch and now that he was touching her, she couldn't take it. She had no chill button. She rode his fingers like they were the real thing.

"You like that?" David moans.

"No, I love it." Three fingers went to four and David was determined to make Chelsey eat her words. He didn't caring if he was hurting her because he knew his wife's limits and there were no limits with Chelsey. She was a true white girl in the bed. She invited pain. Sometimes David wished her vagina was more innocent, but that was a far-fetched dream. Chelsey had the most experienced pussy he had ever had. Her college days were her wildest ones.

"Mommy," Chelsey cuffs David's head between her legs and he comes to a complete halt.

"Yes Chloe, is everything okay?"

"I can't sleep. Can I sleep in here with you?" Torn between a rock and a hard place, Chelsey nods her head yes. It wasn't often that Chloe called her mommy and she just couldn't bring her lips to say no. Slowly, David makes his way to the top of the bed, turns on his side and softly murmurs, *thank you God.*

"I know baby, I'm sorry. Please forgive me." Chelsey assumes David is disappointed in her decision but reality it's the complete opposite. Chloe tucks herself between the two and like an instigator, she turns her parents against one another. Chelsey turns on one side to face the restroom and David turns towards the window. The three attempt to fetch the one hour they have to sleep but Chloe's tossing and turning left David restless.

"Chloe, you're going to have to be still." Chloe wraps her arms around David's waist and rest her head on his back. Then the untimeliest thing happens. David's boxers stiffen. He slides away from Chloe until he's at the end and can't slide anymore, but like a lost puppy, she follows. Uncomfortable, David jumps up from the bed and goes to the kitchen to prep breakfast.

CHAPTER 6

"**A**ttention class, attention class!" The loud little monsters turn their attention towards the front of the classroom and Chloe could feel their eyes burning holes through her face.

"We have a new pirate joining the ship today; do you want to tell everyone your name?" the thin brunette asks Chloe.

"Chloe McCrary...I mean Chloe Winter," she stutters.

"She doesn't even know her own name and she's in the second grade!" a natural blonde, blue-eyed seven year old yells.

"Let's be nice Kathy."

"Are you going to be okay Chloe?" David kneels down to her height.

"Yes, she's going to be just fine," Ms. Hilton answers before Chloe could murmur one word out.

"You just go on to work and I got it from here. It's always harder for kids to get comfortable with new surroundings when the parent is around." Ms. Hilton rushes David out of the classroom, pushing him from the back.

"I promise you; she'll have a mouthful to talk about when she returns." Chloe stands like a mannequin in a shopping store. Surveying the room for a friendly or familiar face, but she couldn't spot any. Everyone seems to be of a different race with an uninviting face.

"Go on Chloe, find a seat anywhere you like. Today we're finger painting." Slowly, Ms. Hilton leads Chloe to the front the desk.

"Have you ever finger painted before?" Slowly, Chloe shakes her head no.

"Well, that's okay, Bella can help you out. Bella would you like to be the teacher's helper today and show Chloe the ropes?"

"No, I'll pass. Thank you," the young girl responds.

"I'll show her the ropes Ms. Hilton!" the little freckle-faced boy with the bowl cut hollers out.

"Great, thank you Johnathan." Hesitantly, Chloe follows Johnathan to the back of the classroom to the book bag cubby.

"What are you? Are you white or are you black?"

"Brianna, that's not the way you ask someone their race. Use your manners."

"Her mother must be black because her hair is kinky," the little girl named Taylor chimes in.

"Black people have nappy hair, so that means her momma's hair was nappy," the third member of the mean girl's clique adds.

"My mommy's hair isn't nappy!" Before Ms. Hilton could chime in and get control of the situation, Chloe charges full-speed at Robin.

"Chloe, no! We don't use our hands to express ourselves, we use our words. Now Robin, you owe Chloe an apology."

"Me owe her an apology?" Robin asks with confusion pasted on her face.

"Yes, an apology. Now please."

"I'm sorry."

"You're sorry for what exactly?"

"I'm sorry for calling your mother's hair nappy."

"Now you go and have a seat. Chloe let me talk to you outside."

****

"A writer never dies. His fears, fantasies….."

"Sorry to interrupt you Professor Winter, but your daughter's school is on the phone for you. They said that it's an emergency and that they couldn't reach your phone," Amanda, David's red-head assistant whispers in his ear.

"I want everybody's memoir in no later than Friday people. Let's look alive, the week is just beginning." The class begins packing up before David could finish his sentence. As soon as the room was clear, he pulls out his phone and dials Ms. Hilton's number off the paper Amanda wrote it down on.

"Hello, can I speak to Ms. Hilton please?"

"Hello, Mr. Winter, this is me. I'm glad you called."

"Is everything okay with Chloe?" he interrupts her to ask.

"She was involved in a fight today. One of the girls joked about her mother's hair and well, Chloe attacked her."

"Bullying is something I do not tolerate Ms. Hilton.."

"No, I completely understand. That's one of…" David denies Ms. Hilton time to explain.

"Chloe witnessed her birth mother's murder and that's a sensitive spot for her." Completely embarrassed, Ms. Hilton allows David to finish before speaking another word.

"I was told this was one of the best schools here in Georgia and that's the main reason she is attending. I'm not paying for her to be bullied, are we clear?"

"Yes we are," Ms. Hilton answers.

"Where is Chloe now?"

"See that's the thing I was calling about. Chloe has been crying since the accident and she's refusing to come back into the classroom. I'm going to need you or Ms. Winter to come up to the school." Irritably David exhale short puffs.

"Someone will be there," he replies before ending the call abruptly. Soon after, he dials Chelsey's number and on the first ring, she answers.

"Is everything okay? I just got to my phone and I see there have been three missed calls from Chloe's school and now I'm not getting in touch with anyone," Chelsey was hysterical.

"Calm down Chelsey. She's fine. However someone needs to go up to the school and get her. She's been crying non-stop."

"Well did they say why she was crying?"

"She attacked a girl for calling her mother's hair nappy and now she refuses to come back into the classroom." Aggressively, Chelsey exhales.

"Shit, I can't leave work for this. We're swamp and short on nurses today."

"I'm less than twenty minutes away from my next class, I can't leave." An awkward silence invades the conversation.

"Shit Chelsey, this is what I was talking about right here! Fuck! I'll go get her!"

****

The ride back home was an awkward one. David didn't know how to talk to kids without saying the wrong thing. It was the very reason why he was a professor and not a teacher. While Clover sang every song on the kids pop CD, Chloe just stares blankly out of the window. Every so often David would peek at her through the mirror to check on her, but he quit when his pants begin to stiffen. Like an untimely police, David's erection pops up.

He jerks on his pants in an attempt to control the rising snake, but it only made his hormones rage. It was days he wished like hell that he would stiffen for Chelsey, but she didn't do it for him anymore. Silently, he begins to pray under the annoying music.

"Dear Lord, I come to you for your help. I'm in need of your strength to fight this disgusting craving. Please, I come to you for a cure. Help me Jesus. Help me God. Amen."

CHAPTER 7

David stretches for the sun before rolling over to spot the time. "Awww, shit!" he exclaimed. "Chelsey, this clock is a piece of shit. It's damn near eight o'clock. I'm never going to make it through that traffic in time for work."

"Oh my God!" Chelsey empathized. "The clock must have stopped during the night. I'm so sorry baby."

David ignores Chelsey's apology and grabs his Tag Heuer watch from the nightstand drawer. "Shit, it'll be nine before I know it," he mumbles, fumbling around the house for missing clothing.

"Let me iron that shirt for you."

"I don't have time for that shit Chelsey!"

Instantly, Chelsey's feelings soften. Tears of sorrow slide down her cheeks. Hearing her sniffling, David sits down on the edge of the bed. "It's all right, Chelsey. It was just a mistake. Don't cry, baby. I'm sorry for yelling." David could not stand to see Chelsey cry and at that very moment he began to feel guilty for blaming her for their over sleeping.

"We just got to get our schedules balanced because I can't have another night like last night. Tackling the household chores and the kids, I didn't get into bed until after midnight and I still haven't gone over my papers," David complained, fastening the buttons on his wrinkled shirt. "I got to go Peaches; my wife is probably worried sick." David jokes, chuckling at the face of the now smiling Chelsey.

He grabs his blazer and heads for the door. "I'll pick up some breakfast on the way. See you."

****

"Mr. Winter, I'm sorry to interrupt."

David was irritated at the sound of his assistant's voice blaring through the intercom. He was sure he made his instructions clear; he was not to be bothered for the next hour. Term papers began to pile up and he was working on little to no sleep. Irritably, he nods his head.

"Yes, Amanda?"

"You have an emergency phone call."

"From whom?"

"Saint Christian Academy. It's about your daughter."

"Mr. Winter? Mr. Winter? Are you there?" Amanda yells into the phone, waking David out of his daze.

"Put them through Amanda." The frustration was real noticeable and Amanda hated being the messenger at such moments.

"David Winters," he answers

"Hello Mr. Winters, I'm sorry to bother you with bad news again but we seem to be having a little problem with Chloe." David had run out of patience with the school and wasn't coy about his frustrations.

"What now?" he asks abruptly.

"Chloe, has locked herself in the supply closet and refuses to come out," Ms. Hilton stutters.

"Can you tell me why she has locked herself into the supply closet, Ms. Hilton?" Silence interrupts the conversation for at least ten seconds before Ms. Hilton responds.

"She said she was picked on by the girls in the bathroom. I'm not sure how true it is or what happened as the girls go to the restroom alone."

"If she said it happened, it happened. I'm on the way."

"Okay," Hilton quickly answered.

"Oh, Ms. Hilton."

"Yes?"

"You might want to gather up the principal and all the other parents because I'm not just coming to get Chloe. I'm coming to get answers." Ms. Hilton could tell from David's tone, that he was livid.

"Sure, I'll make those calls now."

"You do that." As soon as David could get off the phone with Ms. Hilton, he speed dialed Chelsey. After three calls, she finally answers.

"Hello."

"I've called you a million times Chelsey!" he exaggerates.

"I'm sorry, I was in the ER," she explains.

"Answer me this! How are you trying to be a mother, but you're never available for the kids?" Chelsey knew better than to throw gasoline on fire, so she maintained her tone, making sure she didn't upset David any more.

"I'm sorry David, what's going on now?" she asks calmly.

"Chloe has locked herself in the closet. Some girls were bullying her." Angry, Chelsey exhale abruptly.

"Don't worry, I'm about to handle them. This will not happen again but when I get home, we have to talk and I do mean talk. Not bounce around subjects like you like to do." Chelsey's heart speeds up. Everything in her gut said this wasn't good, but she tried her best to shake it off.

"Thanks David, I owe you one. You've been extremely helpful baby daddy and I must reward you," she jokes, failing at lighting the mood.

"I'll see you tonight Chelsey. Bye."

****

The loud laughter echoes from the restroom and David attempts to turn the game up over the noise but the racket increases. *Boom!*

"What are you girls doing in there?" he screams out, but they just burst into laughter.

"Are you bathing or playing?" he asks the girls.

"Bathing," the two of them answer together.

Curious, David grabs the Xfinity security device and zooms in on the bathroom camera to check to see if the girls were bathing. Sure enough, they were playing, singing in a shampoo bottle, bouncing around as if the tub was their stage.

Sickly, David's nature begins to rise. His mind screamed no in three different languages but his body said yes.

"No David. No," he whispers while sliding his hand into his Levi jeans.

"You're so beautiful," he murmurs before choking his penis. And just like that he was back on drugs again. For a long ten minutes, David jerks at his steel. The feeling was better than cooked food. It had been a while since he had a good nut and he couldn't control his hormones. He desperately wanted his nut to come quick but only so he could catch another one.

"Aww, yes. Thank you," he groans, holding the security device in one hand and choking his steel with the other.

"Come on, come on fuck!" he growls before spraying the warm semen all over the device.

"What the hell are you doing?" David's heart drops to his stomach at the sound of Chelsey's voice. He was so into his masturbation that he didn't hear her come in through the kitchen door.

"Oh, look who made it home?" He responds, in an attempt to buy some time.

"Actually, I'm a little early. But you would know that if you weren't in the middle of my seating room masturbating." The closer Chelsey came to David, the more jittery he became.

"Look at you, you have fucking semen everywhere!" she complains before quickly snatching the Xfinity device from David's hand.

"The kids play with this device, you know? Shit. You couldn't go in the fucking room with this shit?" For a quick twenty seconds, David's gut freezes. He knew it was only a matter of seconds before Chelsey looked down at the camera.

"No!" she cries out before dropping to her knees.

"Why David? Why?" tears storm from her eyes and down her cheeks.

Stiff as a mannequin, David just blankly stares at Chelsey as she beats the floor with her fist.

"You promised me. You fucking promised me!" David knew there were no words he could use to comfort Chelsey's pain. So, he slowly fetches the room for his things.

"Did you fucking touch them, you asshole?" Before he could answer, Chelsey's fist pounds into his chest. One time, two times, ten. Punches, kicks, and scratches. Chelsey puts her all into beating David, but he stands firm as a wall for five minutes before grabbing her close.

"I didn't touch them dammit, I swear! This is all your fault; you knew about my situation and yet you choose to surround me with temptation." Chelsey rubs her hands through her messy blonde hair.

"You promised me you were good."

"There's no curing this shit Chelsey!" Warm tears rain from David's glistening eyes.

"I wish like hell this shit wasn't my reality. I fight it every day and I've being doing damn good up until now!" The cracks in the floor squeak as David paces the floor.

"I told you this adoption shit wasn't a good idea, but you still forced it on me."

"We're out the tub now!" Chloe yells out the bathroom door, hoping the sound of her voice would stop the arguing.

"Go into your rooms babies, I'll be in there to tuck you in soon, okay? Let me talk to David for a minute." Chelsey sucked at acting. Chloe could hear the crack in her voice and she knew nothing was as good as she tried to make it sound.

"But we're hungry," Chloe responds.

"You haven't feed them?" Chelsey snaps.

"I was waiting for you to get here so I could order some pizza."

"Just go to your room Chloe and Clover; I'll let you know when the pizza gets here, okay?" Hesitantly, Chloe took Clover's hand and the two went into their room and closed the door behind them.

"I want your sick ass out of my house and out of my life." The words cut a line through Chelsey's gut; she couldn't stomach feeling that way about the only man she's ever loved. A part of her questioned her decision. For years, she and David were good. He hadn't looked at a kid for years. There was a good chance she and David could live happily together, but she would have to live life without ever experiencing the joy of being a mother and that thought scared her more than losing David, so she stuck to her gut.

"I'm sorry for hurting you Chelsey."

"I don't want to hear it David, leave!"

"I'm leaving, I just wanted to let you know that I'm sorry and I never meant to hurt you. You're…" Before David could finish, Chelsey charges at him with full force. She couldn't risk hearing David's apology and good words because she knew deep down he was a good man, just with a sick addiction. His pure heart was the very thing that captured her heart many years ago.

"I don't want hear shit you have to say, just leave. I'll get your things packed and you come and get them when we're gone." Eager to please Chelsey, David, without a second thought, leaves the house. As soon as the door closes, Chelsey breaks down to her knees, crying for hours. Without notice, Chelsey forgets to feed the girls who had sung themselves to sleep.

CHAPTER 8

The loud obnoxious crying sent chills up Chloe's spine. She tosses and turns but fails to open her eyes. "No... no!" she screams as she visualizes the horrific scene of her father with a pistol to her mother's head. "Don't shoot her, please, don't shoot her!" Chloe's heart rattles with the shaky walls after Chelsey slams the Xfinity device into the wall with force.

"Noooooo!" Finally Chloe jumps up out of her sleep.

"It's okay Chloe, it's okay!" Chelsey bursts into the room and says.

"I'm here, it's okay." Chelsey wraps her arms around Chloe and rests her head onto her chest while rubbing her fingers through her kinky curls.

"Are you okay mommy?" The word "mommy" coming from Chloe lights a fire in Chelsey's gut she never knew existed. The feeling was overwhelming.

"Yes baby, why wouldn't I be?"

"I don't know, but your heart is pounding like African drums." Chelsey chuckles at Chloe's response.

"I'm just happy, that's all." A tear slowly rains from Chelsey's eye.

"Why are you happy, because David's gone?"

"No, because I know now choosing to be your mother wasn't a mistake."

"Mommy, we never ate," Clover interrupted and said.

"I'm sorry girls, mommy had to let out some stress but I promise I'm all yours now." The girls hug Chelsey's waist tight like a coat.

"Is David gone for good?" Chloe asks.

"Yes baby, it'll just be us from now on."

"But why?" Chloe questions.

"Things between David and me just didn't work out." The crack in Chelsey's voice made Chloe even more curious, but she didn't want to make Chelsey cry, so she changes the subject.

"Okay, well can we order that pizza now?" Chloe's hazel eyes lock with Chelsey's icy blues eyes and the two just smile.

"Yes, let's order pizza and binge out in front of the television."

"What does binge out mean?" Clover asks Chelsey.

"Eat snacks and fall asleep in front of the television."

"Oh, that's sounds good to me!"

****

"Oh my goodness, look at that Chloe!" the 47,000 pound whale shark was stunning up close. The girls couldn't believe their eyes. They were in awe of the beautiful and ugly fishes at Georgia's aquarium, the largest in the world. They hardly paid any attention to Jessica and Chelsey the entire time.

"I'm so scared I don't know what to do Jessica. How am I supposed to raise two kids on my own?"

"You just get it done, that's how. You just be glad you caught him when you did Chelsey." Chelsey was sure that she was doing the right thing but her heart was still yearning for David. He was the only man she loved for the last fourteen years. No matter how bad the situation was, she just couldn't turn off her love for him like a light switch.

"I don't think he would have touched them Jessica." "You don't know." Jessica's eyes search for the girls before finishing her sentence. She needed to make sure they weren't listening to her next words.

"You don't know what that damn would have done to them girls!"

"Would you keep your damn voice down?" Chelsey whispers, watching the girls eat their cotton candy, pounding on the tanks at the fishes.

"You better not be thinking about that damn monster Chelsey!" A web of tears form in the corner of Chelsey's icy blue eyes and instantly Jessica's heart melts.

"I can't just turn off my love for him Jessica. So, go ahead and tell me you told me so." Jessica didn't want Chelsey to break down in front of the kids, so she holds back her opinions and holds her sister tight.

"I'm here for you Chelsey. Now get it together, you got two girls depending on you." Jessica's comfort was everything to Chelsey, since she knew Jessica had a million not so nice words lined up for her.

"Momma, momma, did you see that?" Clover's nails claw at Chelsey's Levi jeans as she tugs her towards the tank.

"Wow, I think it's going to take me a while to get used to hearing you be called momma." The sisters chuckle as they follow the girls to the tank.

"I know, I said the same thing."

"How does it feel to be a mother?"

"It feels scary, I'm tired all the time, I mean I'm just overwhelmed." Jessica's loud silly laughter carries throughout the aquarium. She laughs so hard the girls join just because her laughter is funny.

"Welcome to motherhood sister."

CHAPTER 9

Year 2014

"**I**'m tired of your ass teasing me." Clover quickly reads her text then locks eyes with Aubrey O'Day, the Jaguars' quarterback. He was above average height, about six-three, and all the girls, popular and nerds, described him as *fine as hell*. He and Clover's eyes lock. She sat at a table across the room from where he was standing at a bookcase flipping through some pages. His eyes seem to have a passion burning inside them and she could feel her panties becoming damp from the growing desire to feel him inside her.

She crosses her legs and moves them back and forth, creating a light friction against her vagina, making her desire even more intense. Clover doesn't realize she's sucking on the eraser of the pencil until she follows Aubrey's eyes to her mouth. She then moved her eyes from his face down to the bulge of his pants, and for what seems like an endless moment, she stares at his large print. He breaks the stare with a chuckle. Embarrassed, Clover quickly looks back down to her economics book she was studying for a brief moment, contemplating on her next move.

When she looks back up and he's gone she panics, scanning the library quickly, until she notices him getting in the elevator. Aubrey smiles at Clover as the doors close and something in her explodes. For four months now, she and Aubrey flirted with danger. They didn't bother ignoring their chemistry for the sake of their best friends. Kelly and Tristian were the least of their worries.

Meet me in the library basement.

Clover's heartrate increases as she reads the text. Smoothly, she gets up from the table, grabs her books, coat, and purse and struts out the back exit door, heels clicking down the steps. She reaches ground level and scans the basement like a lost puppy. The elevator is empty, and there was no Aubrey in sight. *What kind of games he playing*, she thought as she continues to scan the room for his gold Jaguar jacket. After concluding he wasn't there, she turns around to fetch the elevator, with disappointment in her heart. Clover looks up and Aubrey is standing right there. In fact, she bumps right into his chest. She could feel her heart pounding as he looks deep into her eyes, up close and personal.

He opens his mouth to say something, probably to ask her a time buying question, but she puts her finger over his lips. She knew talking would only ruin the mood. Clover ignores her shattered nerves and leads Aubrey to the back of the library basement where stacks of books were piled up on tables. Following her lead, he lifts her up onto the table, then she takes his hand and placed it between her legs.

"What about Kelly and Tristian?"

"What about them?" she whispers into his ear before his fingers pushed the crotch of her body suit and panties aside and explore her wetness.

"Um," she moans at his touch.

"You're all kinds of bad Clover. Kelly is going to kill you."

"What she doesn't know, won't hurt her." Clover was no longer Chelsey's baby girl; she was all grown up. In a couple of months she will be graduating and finally, out of her mother's house and free of her overbearing rules.

Aubrey brings his face closer to Clover and the two's tongues wrestle. Clover's sassiness did something to Aubrey, and surprisingly he was about to give Clover what every boy in the school wanted to give her, the business and he didn't even need a room. He picks her up with her legs straddled around his back and carries her to the far back where an empty table awaits them. As soon as she is down, her their clothes come off quickly. Both of them ripping at the other until they were completely naked in the dimly lit room.

Experienced, she takes her finger and rubs it against her clit, taking it and putting it into his mouth, letting him savor her juice off of it. She rubs her finger against her clit again, this time sucking her own juice off her finger.

"Damn Clover, you're a beast girl."

"Do you think you can keep up?" she teases before the two begin to kiss, both savoring her sweetness at the same time. He pushes her back on the desk so that her head was hanging over the rear and her nipples were protruding upward into the air. He suckles on them one at a time, taking her small pearls into his mouth and licking the entire breast. Starting at the base of each one with the tip of his tongue and making light, circular strokes until he reaches the hardened prize. She was in ecstasy. She and Kelly had spent many days speaking about Aubrey's sex.

Tristian is a virgin, and for a minute, Clover flirted with the idea of being his first. She even got a kick out of tooting her nose up at Kelly the days she would speak about she and Aubrey's sex plays. The entire time she would secretly fantasize about it being her Aubrey was satisfying.

Aubrey takes both of Clover's breasts, one in each hand, pushes them together and then sweeps both nipples into his mouth at the same time. Her moan grow intense. Still palming her breasts, he makes a trail with his tongue down to her belly button, pausing just long enough to take a quick dip into it before moving down to explore between her thighs. Before Clover could even prepare herself for what was about to come, Aubrey takes her hardened clit into his mouth and begins to let it vibrate on the tip of his tongue.

"This is my first time baby; do you like it?" Aubrey comes up to ask.

"Ohh, you're good baby, show me you want it." Clover was different from the other young girls Aubrey made out with. She was like an experienced cougar. He loved every minute of her dirty talking. He continues to eat her pussy for the next fifteen minutes or so, and she comes at least five to six times in his mouth. After eating her for what seems like an eternity, he walks around to the other side of the desk, where her head is hanging over the side. Clover comes face to face with Aubrey's delicious-looking dick. She hesitates not for a second and takes the head of it into her mouth with a heightened desire to know what he tastes like in reality and not a fantasy.

And there, with her head upside down, she sucks on a dick for the very first time. It was heaven. Clover holds the base of it while he dick feeds her, pushing his manhood in and out of her mouth with increasing speed.

"Relax baby, so you can get it all in."

She relaxes her throat like a professional and he eventually gets it all in. She loves every minute of it; he loves every minute of it. The two are so into each other they don't hear the librarian, Ms. Batter, enter the room.

"Oh my goodness, what are you two doing in here?" It was very clear what the two teens were doing but Ms. Batter couldn't believe her eyes. Ten years she worked for the school system and never had she seen kids sexing like porn stars. Quickly, Aubrey jerks his penis from Clover's mouth. The two jump and search for their clothes.

"You two put on your clothes and meet me in the principal's office!" Ms. Batter yells out with her hands over her eyes. As soon as the room is clear, Aubrey bursts into laughter.

"I guess she's going to be next in line since now she knows what the snake hit like," he jokes, zipping up his black Ralph Lauren jeans.

"You stupid Aubrey, damn she just had to interrupt." As embarrassed as Clover was, she was still mad she didn't get to feel Aubrey inside of her.

"Fuck that, I'll be at your window like Ole boy in Love and Basketball tonight." Aubrey and Clover's giggling echoes out into the hallway.

"Hey, hurry up in there!" Ms. Batters screams out beating on the door.

"Honey we coming, you don't have to sit there and wait on us," Clover sasses.

"I heard that Miss Clover."

"I know Ms. Batter."

CHAPTER 10

"I just can't believe you Clover; I didn't raise you this way!" Chelsey swerves in and out of lanes with intense speed.

"Momma, I wish you would slow down? Dang, it's really not that serious. You're overreacting per usual."

"Do you know what I wish for Clover? Do you?" she asks turning her attention on Clover.

"Momma, look at the road! Oh my God! You're going to kill us!"

"Oh don't you bring God into this misses!" she spazzes out while running her free hand through her blonde bob.

"Like seriously Clover, what's going on with you?" Like clockwork, Clover's water works begin.

"I'm not going for the puppy dog tears anymore. Clearly, you're a big girl now." Tears slowly drip from Clover's beautiful hazel eyes.

"Having sex wasn't good enough for you; you had to have ORAL sex in school and with your BEST FRIEND'S boyfriend! Clover!"

"What? Dammit, shit! I fucked up, okay? I fucked up! Are you happy now?" Clover's harsh tone sends chills up Chelsey's spine. She knew she bit off a big chunk when she adopted the girls but nothing could prepare her for the teen era.

"You're right Clover, you fucked up. Now it's time you get a taste of the real world. So from now on, what you do is your business. You're officially grown in my eyes." The calmness in Chelsey's voice shoots fear into Clover's guts.

"A little advice baby girl, your past stays with you. It's never erased. Good Luck." Slowly, Chelsey pulls in the driveway to her dream home. Though it had been over six years since Chelsey had seen or even spoken to David, his alimony checks never stopped. He was a man of his word and he gave Chelsey his word that he would continue to provide for her and the girls until she was remarried.

"I'm sorry," Clover breaks the silence and says.

"You're sorry for what Clover?" Chelsey scrambles through her junky purse for her singing phone.

"I'm sorry for disappointing you and letting you down. I know you wish I was more like Chloe." Chelsey ignores the crack in Clover's voice.

"I've never asked you to live your life to please me or to be like your sister. You didn't let me down; you let yourself down. You'll be graduating very soon Clover, it's time you get it together," she responds dryly before answering her phone.

"Hey Jessica," Chelsey answers irritably.

"Is everything okay with Clover? Is she okay?"

"Yes she's fine. We'll talk later."

"You don't have to wait until I'm gone to talk about me, go ahead and do what you do best. Run your mouth," Clover spazzes out before slamming the door on the Honda. Clover was mad all over again. She couldn't stand not getting her way, and for the very first time, Chelsey was sticking to her guns. Clover's puppy dog tears and soft apology was usually all she needed to win Chelsey back over to her side, but not this time.

"What was that about?" Jessica asks.

"Sister, I think I'm about to have a nervous breakdown. I got one daughter calling home every week threating to leave school and the other giving out oral in school. Where did I go wrong?"

"You can't blame yourself for their decisions, plus they're growing young ladies, what did you expect?"

"I didn't expect it to be this hard, that's for…"

"Hold up, wait a minute! What did you say Clover did?" Jessica asks, after replaying Chelsey's complaints in her head.

"Yes, you heard me right; she was caught in the library basement giving her best friend's boyfriend oral sex."

"Are you talking about Kelly, Chelsey?"

"Yes, the only friend she has left."

"Oh my, that little Aubrey is something else."

"How do you know him?"

"Chelsey, who don't know him?"

"Me."

"All the little girls want that boy. He tried getting at your niece but she wasn't having it." Chelsey exhales abruptly.

"See, that's what I'm talking about. How did you get my nieces in line?"

"I told you, you got to give them space and let them open up to you. Anyway, enough about these kids, I called you for something else." Chelsey snatches the phone from her ear and eyes the caller I.D. as if she could see Jessica through the phone. It was very rare for Jessica to call her for something. She took the big sister role seriously. She didn't believe in asking Chelsey for anything.

"What could I possible do for you my love?" Chelsey jokes.

"Will you stop playing?" Jessica responds.

"Okay, what is it?"

"Can you pleaseeee... Never mind."

"Will you stop acting like these damn kids and ask me already!"

"Will you go out on a double date with me?" Chelsey's silence was all the answer Jessica needed.

"See, that's okay. Forget I asked."

"I didn't say no you big baby, I'm just curious on who you're trying to set me up with, that's all. "

"Can I just get one blind yes? If I get it wrong, you get to tell me every day for the rest of our lives."

"Yes."

****

"Most people appear slightly different from their picture but she looks pleasantly the same. Even better actually, good job Robier." Chelsey's blind date murmurs into Jessica's husband's ear before the two of them walk towards the girls.

"Girl, isn't he fine?" Jessica whispers as they walk closer to the guys.

"He's okay; we'll see how fine he is when the night is over."

"Just promise to be open Chelsey," Jessica murmurs before they reached the guys.

"Hello beautiful," Thomas greets Chelsey with a warm, inviting smile.

Just call me by my name man, Chelsey thought before responding, "Hey, how are you?"

"I'm doing better now that I'm here with you." Instantly, Chelsey's attitude begins to sour. Thomas' game talk was quickly becoming irritating.

"I already wrote our names down, so we can just sit over here on the benches until they call our names," Robier adds, leading the gang to the benches outside the steakhouse. The wait for the table was more than an hour. Thomas purposely snuggles up next to Chelsey on one of the benches while they listen to the waiters yell out party names. They weren't modernized enough to have those hand buzzers many restaurants use today, so every few minutes, a country voice yells out someone's name. For the first ten minutes, Chelsey uses listening out for their names as an excuse to cut conversations short.

She just wasn't into dating that much. Out of the twelve years David had been gone, she had only been with three guys; one who she didn't bother sleeping with after accidently seeing his small penis. She and David had hooked up with each other a couple of times for the first two years of their split before coming to a completely stop.

"Jones, party of four." Chelsey turns her attention towards the restaurant door, trying her hardest to avoid eye contact with Thomas.

"I didn't think it was humanly possible for someone to look ten times better than their pictures," Thomas breaks the silence and says.

"Thanks, you're not so bad yourself," Chelsey observes Thomas complete look and surprisingly Jessica had did a good job at picking a good looking date. Thomas' clean cut and perfectly lined beard caught Chelsey's eye. He was over six feet and nicely built to match the height, but Thomas was going to need more than good looks to capture Chelsey's heart. She was used to smart, calm men.

"Am I what you expected?" Thomas asks.

"I didn't expect a particular person. In fact, I was unsure what to expect with Jessica being the match maker." For the first time of night, the two share a laugh. Jessica's eyes Chelsey and Thomas curiously from across the walkway, where she and Robier waited on the opposite side on a bench.

"Well hopefully I didn't disappoint you."

"Oh no, it could have been much worse. I had all kinds of nightmares before today," Chelsey jokes and the two once again chime in on some good ole laughter.

"Smith party of four." Forty-five minutes had blown by quickly once Chelsey let her guard down a little.

"Oh that's us yawl." Robier jumps up and leads the crowd into the steakhouse. Dinner goes off without a hitch. Everyone fills their bellies with oversized steaks, stuffed baked potatoes, and gigantic salads. Chelsey had promised Thomas that it wouldn't be the last time he saw her but she wasn't able to give him a date on their next meet and greet. He attempts to kiss her but she respectfully shuts him down and assures him, if ever he should get in the gate, it will be worth his while.

CHAPTER II

"Welcome back!" Clover had been waiting for Chloe by the window all day. She was excited about their night in. Chloe was back from school and Clover was ready to catch up.

"You came prepared I see." Chloe came dressed in her large, faded tie dye t-shirt, ready for the pajama party.

"Hey baby, I miss you so much!" Chelsey charged Chloe with her arms spread wide. The two hugged swaying back and forth for a long twenty seconds.

"I miss you guys so much." Chloe ran over to Clover and bear hugged her tight.

"You've done something with your hair or maybe it's just your eyes." Chloe lit up the room.

"Yeah, I straightened my hair." Chloe bounced her freshly ironed wrap.

"It looks good on you Chloe." Chelsey is happy to see Chloe. They were more like best friends than momma and daughter.

"Let's get this party started right!" Clover yelled out turning up the radio.

"I like this song." Chloe joins Clover and the two dance in the floor like they were at the hottest club in Atlanta.

"Are you ready to graduate?" Chloe yelled over the roar of music.

"What you say?" A distant hazy chatter could be heard, but Clover couldn't make out what Chloe was saying.

"Are you ready to graduate?" Clover still couldn't make out what Chloe was saying to be exact but she knew she heard her say graduate, so she nods her head *yes*. The two laugh in unison and the laughter wouldn't seem to stop. The song got louder, pulling them in more and more into the groove. Chelsey couldn't help herself, she joins the girls, jumping in a huddle group like Tic -Tacs being shaken in a box; after dancing and eating, the girls whine down to catch up on lost time and current gossip.

"So, Chloe is this new glow coming from a new lover?"

"No, I still got my V-card." Clover rolls her eyes at Chelsey's over dramatic applauds.

"Well I'm glad somebody still does," Chelsey adds.

"What? Are you telling me you're not pure anymore?"

"No, she's very experienced," Chelsey joked.

"Do tell, do tell!" Chloe props up on Chelsey's queen sized-bed positioning for the tea.

"Well to be honest, I've been started. So that little bit momma saw was nothing." Chloe's forehead wrinkles.

"What you mean the time momma *saw?* What did momma see?" Clover chuckles shying her attention away from Chloe.

"Momma what did you see?" Chelsey shakes her head in disgust.

"You don't want to know."

"No, trust me I do." Chloe was eager to know the tea.

"Honey, me and Aubrey did a little exercise in the library basement," Clover jokes.

"Oh my goodness Clover, are you serious right now?" Clover couldn't face Chloe. She jumps up from the bed full of laughter.

"They were doing a little more than exercise," Chelsey adds. Chloe's ears ring like grenades had been thrown.

"What were you doing Clover?"

"She was giving oral."

"What are you doing giving head to your best friend's man Clover? That's just too much now."

"I'm glad someone agrees." Chelsey was relieved that it wasn't just her that felt Chloe's actions were wrong.

"Enough about me, let's hear about you and this date." Clover aims the attention on Chelsey.

"Oh, you two just have been off the chain," Chloe adds.

"Nothing happened, it was just a date. I haven't been active in a while. Honestly, I do need some but I'm not in a rush."

"Both of you need to get laid," Clover chimes in.

"I can't believe you haven't had sex yet Chloe. You're a twenty-something virgin." Chelsey joins Clover in laughter.

"Well everybody can't be like you Ms. Thing." Chloe meant her words, as she was nothing like Clover. She was thin, short and still favored a junior high school kid. Nothing about her body had matured. Meanwhile, Clover looked over twenty in the body. No one would know she was still in high school if she didn't tell them.

"Don't worry, I got you tomorrow sister. There will be some cute boys at the graduation. I'll hook you up; maybe we can even go on a double date." Chloe frowns at the thought.

"I don't want you to throw your life away like your momma over here. She can't seem to get over... what's his name again?" Clover jokes, speaking of David.

"She's right, as much as I hate to say it. You got to get out your skin Chloe." Clover nods in agreeance with her lips pucker out.

"My ideas always work, sometimes," Clover jokes before the girls fixate their attention back on their favorite movie, "Pretty Woman." Twenty minutes in, Clover was out for the night.

"I ought to mess with her," Chloe turns and says to Chelsey.

"Please don't, you know how that girl's attitude is when she is awakened from her sleep. So, how long do I have you for?" Chloe knew

Chelsey would eventually ask her routine question, so she was prepared and very anxious to drop the bomb on her.

"You have me forever." Chelsey squints her eyes low and turns her full body around to Chloe.

"What are you talking about?"

"I'm not going back momma. I'm miserable up there. Besides, I want to be here with you and Clover. I've missed so much being gone."

"Chloe, that's not a good enough reason to drop out of school. A school your daddy pulled crazy strings to get you in." Instantly, Chloe's tone changes from sweet and innocent to sassy and unappreciative.

"First off, he's not our daddy. We haven't even seen that man since he left out of the blue. Secondly, I don't want to be a doctor anymore, I've changed my major to writing and I've enrolled in Georgia State." Chelsey wasn't used to Chloe having such a fiery tone with her, so she just sat and listened. She could tell that Chloe was very serious from the pitch in her voice.

"It's my life and you can't live it for me." Chloe's increased tone didn't bother Clover a bit; she slept right through the debate.

"No, I would never try and live your life for you Chloe but I'm your mother and mothers help their daughters out when they come upon a difficult decision like this. I thought maybe you would at least consider running this by me before deciding."

"I would have but I knew you would just try and change my mind and I've made my mind up." Instead of trying to convince Chloe she was making a horrible mistake, Chelsey just walked over to Chloe and hugged her tightly.

"I support you; I want nothing more than to have you here with me." Chelsey's words were comforting and Chloe just burst into tears, sobbing.

"I miss yawl so much and I just didn't fit in there. Life was becoming stressful." Chelsey's next question was answered. She was curious to know how Chloe's social life was working out for her in school.

"Don't cry I'm happy you're home. It's going to be fun, just watch. I'm not going to know how to act with both of my girls home."

CHAPTER 12

"It's finally here; the moment of truth, the stepping stone to the real world," Chloe mumbles as she packs layers of makeup on her naturally beautiful face.

"Yes, I've been preparing you for this day for thirteen years." Chelsey dab's her eyes with her handkerchief.

"Momma, don't you start that. I'm going to send you out of here." Clover was moments away from being free and she wanted to soak in the moment without Chelsey stealing the show with her tears.

"I'm going to miss high school, the good, bad, idiotic, fun and challenging times."

"Trust me, you won't think about it anymore for years once you walk across that stage." Chloe admired Clover's beauty through the mirror she fixed her makeup in.

"Well momma, let's go grab our seats, I think she's got it from here."

"I'll see yawl in a minute."

****

Clover grew nervous as it was time for her to step out in the bright light. She tried to avoid shaking hands with the administrator as her palms were sweaty but he insists. Quickly, she grabs her ticket of freedom and marches off the stage.

"Momma I did it!" she yells before charging Chloe, Chelsey, and her aunt Jessica. She waves the piece of paper that will forever remind her that she accomplished something in the air like it was money.

"I'm so proud of you Clover." Aunt Jessica bear hugs Clover, stamping her red lipstick on her cheeks as they sway side-to-side.

"Thank you Aunt." After twenty long seconds, Clover breaks loose from her Aunt's hug and then walks over to Chloe and murmurs.

"Remember what we talked about?" Chloe looks confused until she spots the two college boys winking their eyes at her and Clover.

"Oh my goodness, Clover what did you tell them?" Chloe asks, avoiding the boy's eyes.

"Oh relax, I got this. I know what to say and what not to say." And without a second thought, Chloe let it be. She had trust in Clover's approach, after all, it was the one thing she did best; *boys*. Chelsey treated the girls to lunch at Benihana so they wouldn't come off as greedy girls on their dates, and then they did a little shopping for Chloe's sake.

****

The girls all watched as Chloe made her way down the staircase. The scene was like a scene in a movie and Chloe was the princess. For the first time as an adult, Chloe looks seductive, mature and beautiful all at once. Her face was somewhat luminous; her tone glowing. Her eyes were a vibrant shade of brown and her eyebrows were arched to perfection.

"Wow sister, I did a damn good job on you!" Chloe spins around like a store mannequin and almost trips in the four inch heels she borrowed from Clover.

"Woah, well you get the picture," Chloe jokes as she shows off her curve-hugging, teal, bodycon dress.

"Wow Chloe, you ought to dress like this more often."

"Well thanks mom, I thought I dressed perfect for my age." *It's nothing wrong with the way you dress baby, you dress perfect for your age*, were Chelsey's exact words when Chloe complained to her about not having style like Clover.

"Oh you know what I mean. You look beautiful." The soft taps at the door grab the girl's attention and they all turn towards the door.

"Oh they're early," Clover murmurs as she irons the invisible wrinkle out of her cocktail dress.

"Coming!" Chelsey yells out on her way to the door.

"Hey gentlemen, come in." Clover had an eye for candy. Her taste in men was sweet. Jeremy, the guy for Chloe was delicious. His slacks fit his firm waist nicely and his feet weren't covered in tennis, but Steve Madden shoes. Clover had put the date together and she was very specific on what the boys should wear.

"Well, Jeremey, this is my older sister Chloe and Chloe, this is Lloyd's friend Jeremey." Chloe couldn't get control of her nerves.

"Wow, you look even better up close," Jeremey jokes.

"I told you my sister was a hottie."

"Are you ready to make the city jealous?" Chloe twirls her mousy copper hair and stutters.

"Yeah, I guess." Her eyes fixated on Jeremey's attire.

"Your sister got us dressed like we about to go cut a rug or something, so that's why I'm dressed as such." Chloe secretly admired the way Jeremey's body bursts out of his button down. She didn't understand why he was explaining his choice of fashion because he got it *all* right. Her mind was saying, *baby you're perfect*, but her mouth wouldn't utter the words. So instead, she stands there in a daze, starring at his perfectly built body.

"Well, actually, we are going to cut a rug," Clover chimes in.

"Leave it to you to pick out something corny as hell. What you got us doing girl?" Lloyd was Clover's college boo. She met him during a college tour and they've been kicking it since.

"Chill muscle man, we're going dancing."

"I hope pole dancing," Jeremey chimes in following Clover and Lloyd out the door. After twenty long, awkward minutes, the quad arrives at Dance 4-11 studio. Curious, Lloyd instantly reads the description of dance by their name as they sign in.

"Man, Chloe, I'm going to kill you girl." Instantly she bursts into laughter.

"You got to live a little man." Nosy, Jeremey follow suit and reads the dance description.

"Salsa?" Chloe's heart drops. She knew nothing about dancing, let alone being sexy, and salsa was the sexiest dance to date. *I could kill Clover*, she thought as she fidgets in the overly-sexy bodycon dress.

"Sometimes you have to leap before you look. I think we should do insane, irrational things. I think sometimes we should feel ridiculous doing crazy things. Let's leap before we look tonight yawl." Clover's speech had the boys rowdy. They were ready to make fools of themselves, but Chloe couldn't get in the spirit. Her nerves were getting the best of her and she could barely keep her balance in the uncomfortable heels.

"Right this way you guys." Chloe slowly follows behind as the receptionist leads the group into the room. Chloe shyly steps into the salsa dancing class with her feet trembling in her heels. She silently prays, *please don't fall, please don't fall*.

"Okay everyone grab your partner," a high-yellow broad with silky, long, Brazilian hair down to her buttocks quickly grabs Jeremey by the arm.

"Um, excuse me, but he's taken," Clover cuts in and says.

"Sorry baby, maybe next time," Jeremey jokes before grabbing Chloe by the arm.

"Loosen up girl, we got this." Chloe cracked a stale smile then fixated her attention back on the instructor. She tries to remember the moves before the instructor said go, but Jeremey was knocking her off her concentration with his charming jokes.

"Men you are to lead your partners and ladies you are to follow. Let the beat guide your moves and the chemistry spark your style." Like a professional, Jeremey guides Chloe with little tugs, then pushes and at the right moment, he tries to dip Chloe but her feet were killing her and her balance was off.

"Oh, I'm sorry! Are you okay?" Jeremy asks as he pulls Chloe up from almost mopping the floor.

"Yeah, I'm okay. I think I'll just sit this one out." Embarrassed, Chloe hops on her crammed feet to the seats by the wall. And like a running faucet, Jeremy went on with the show. He and Ms. High Yellow tangle like they're on "Dancing with the Stars." Clover and Lloyd try to keep up, but the two were like a match made in heaven. Chloe couldn't stand watching, so she pretends to be sick and rushes off to the rest room.

"Hey Clover, let your sister know I had to run," Jeremy leans over to Clover and whisper as she and Lloyd salsa through the crowd.

"Where are you going bra?" Jeremey gives Lloyd one wink and instantly he is filled in.

"I got you, say no more." Jeremy and little Ms. High Yellow waltz out the dance room, giggling while holding onto each other's arms.

"What about your date?" Chloe hears the girl say from the restroom. At the sound of Jeremy's voice she peeks out the door just to be sure it was really Jeremy with another girl.

"Oh, we not together," Jeremey replies. Chloe's heart sinks as she watches her date skip out on her with a thottie. She prances back into the room with a pasted smile like nothing ever happened.

"Oh, Jeremey had to leave, he had emergency come up." Chloe nods at Clover and responds.

"That's fine, I'm good. Now get back out there and leap before you look," Clover giggles at Chloe's joke and then slides right back onto the dance floor.

CHAPTER 13

A faint hint of laugher mixed with a little of Trey Songz's "I Bet the Neighbors Know My Name" escapes the crack of Clover's room door. Because of the music, Clover and Lloyd don't hear Chloe's light footsteps descending across the hall. She tries to make it to her room without interrupting the two. The last thing she need is them to cut their night short because she has no one. Chelsey was out with Jessica and she just wanted to enjoy the rest of her night in bed with snacks.

Three doughnuts, a bag of salty potato chips and a snicker later, Chloe was interrupted by the moans from the room over. Clover sounds like she was on the ride of her life. Chloe tries to dig her head deep into the soft fluffy white pillows to block out the noise, but nothing works. She tosses back and forth with her leg hanging from underneath the covers until she couldn't take it anymore. She imagines Lloyd's voice to be her favorite romantic hero, Red Butler. Instantly, his voice wets her vagina. Chloe fantasizes about Red Butler invading her sweet walls as Lloyd's groans increase. She had been daydreaming about dick more often than usual lately and the night out with Jeremy made matters worse. She was in heat. She tries to go to sleep but can't because she was horny as hell. So she masturbates off the sweet sounds of Clover and Lloyd love making.

****

Chloe pushes her glasses up on her nose, they magnify her beautiful, brown eyes. Then she twirls her mousy brown hair on her fingers trying to find her angle in the mirror. She was tired of her faults affecting her social skills, she was always at the top of her class, but now she wanted to get on top of her social life.

"I can be your walking dream or your living fantasy." The words sounded stupid rolling off her tongue but Chloe cited them, twirling around in the mirror. She once overheard Clover telling a boy that over the phone.

"Girl you got this, you the shit." Chloe snatches her glasses from her face in search of her natural beauty. She wanted to see what Chelsey and Clover had seen in her. They were always drowning her with beautiful complements, so she searches for her best angles in hope that it will spike up her confidence.

"Chloe you're beautiful. Chloe you're amazing, Chloe, you're the shit." Silently, Chelsey watches Chloe chant to herself in the mirror.

"Oh my goodness, get out!" Startled, Chloe almost jumps out of her skin and slams the restroom door in Chelsey's face. Embarrassed, she breaks down to her knees and bursts into sobbing. She felt even worse than before her pick-me-up chants.

"Chloe, I'm sorry. Open the door please." Chelsey's beating on the door increases as Chloe's sobbing gets louder.

"Go away," she whimpers out.

"Chloe, what's going on with you?" Chloe watches as the door knob on the door turns. Chelsey finally decides to use the bathroom spare key.

"I don't get what's going on."

"I'm tired of being the smart kid. I want to have fun; I want a man. I need a social life. You just don't understand."

"So make me Chloe, because everything you've named, you can have. It's not something to cry about."

"It's not that easy, if it was, I'd be doing it already."

"Chloe you're being silly. You're smart, you're beautiful and you're young. You have your whole life ahead of you."

"You say I'm beautiful because I'm your child. You have to say that, but the boys don't seem to think so. Why am I still single if that's the case?"

"So this is what this about. Clover told me what happened yesterday and Chloe to be honest that could have happened with the most popular girl in America." Chloe's crying intensifies as she realizes Clover and Chelsey had been discussing her.

"Your problem is not with boys liking you but with you liking yourself. Maybe you should go see a therapist. I'll call Savannah tomorrow if you're interested." Chelsey's moist lips peck Chloe on the top of her forehead.

"Now, I got to go to work. Are you going to be okay?" Chelsey slides back out the door after Chloe nods yes.

Chapter 14

End of summer 2014

"Why can't I find happiness? Why are my mood swings so unpredictable?" It was evident in the way Chloe struggles to breathe that her soul was lost. Her chest heaves up and down as she drills the therapist with questions.

"Why do you think your mood swings are unpredictable?" Chloe tries to control her emotions but fails miserably.

"If I knew, I wouldn't be here with you, now would I?" Tears pour from her eyes as she rocks back and forth on Savannah's couch. She fixates her attention on the decorated degrees mounted high on the walls to keep from eyeing her therapist.

"The truth is always rooted deep down in our gut; we just choose to ignore it for whatever reason. Again, I ask, why do you believe you can't find happiness Chloe?" As soothing as Savannah's tone was, Chloe couldn't find her comfort zone. She rocks back and forth with her arms crossed. She wasn't quite ready to face her horrific memories and uneasy thoughts but she knew deep down inside that Savannah was right. *The truth was always available, it's just up to you to use it or not.*

Chloe had prolonged seeing a therapist all summer because she couldn't stomach tackling her true feelings. But a large part of her wants to get better and find her happy medium, so she decided to try it out. Had she known her first session would get so intense so quick, she would have probably prolonged the session's some more.

"I'm not ready for this," she whimpers, before jumping up reach for the door.

"It's okay Chloe, we don't have to cover everything at once but before you leave can you do one thing for me?" Chloe stops her footsteps at the door and listens out for Savannah's favor.

"I want you to start a diary and journal your feelings for me. When you're happy, pen that moment and add what it was that made you happy, and when you're sad do the same. When you're lonely, pen that moment and then add some things that would fulfill your loneliness. Can you do that for me?" Tears slowly drip down Chloe's chin as she nods in agreeance.

"Good. I'll see you at our next scheduled session, won't I?"

"Yes," Chloe murmurs with a crack in her voice.

****

The seating room's windows tremble after Chloe slams the door shut. Weak, Chelsey jumps up from the couch out of her cat nap.

"What's wrong with you now Chloe?" She could barely speak her body was experiencing so much pain.

"I should have never listened to you, that's what's wrong with me."

"I take it your therapy session didn't go as planned."

"No as of matter of fact, it didn't. I've never been so humiliated in my entire life. Do you know how it feels to sit there and cry in front of a complete stranger?" Clover follows the trail of noise to the living room and finds that it is indeed Chloe yet again snapping off on Chelsey.

"As of matter fact, I do Chloe. Yes, I know how it feels. That is the very reason you go to therapy. So you can talk to a stranger who wouldn't judge your feelings or your fucked up life!" For the first time all summer, Chelsey's tone was different. It was filled with anger and a whole lot of command.

"You're just a little spoiled brat who whines about everything. You run around here wanting sympathy from every damn body and when they give it to you, you're still not satisfied." Chloe's facial expression said it all. She couldn't believe Chelsey's tone.

"Damn, you really pissed her off," Clover murmurs after Chelsey disappears up the staircase.

"She's been so grouchy these last couple of days," Chloe responds with a confused daze.

"I don't know Chloe; you've been giving her hell lately sister."

"I know, I don't know what's wrong with me."

"Maybe you just need to go out. Let's go shopping and get some things for school."

"Shopping doesn't solve everything Clover."

"Yeah, but it solves almost everything," Clover jokes before snatching her car keys from the coffee table.

"Come on; let's go let our hair down a little," and like a lost puppy Chloe follows her little sister out the door.

CHAPTER 15

Lenox was packed from wall to wall. Clover moves through the crowd like a diva, getting closer to other people than she usually would like but she knew Chloe needed to get out and her normal internet shopping wasn't going to do it. The messages and carefully styled images to seduce consumers were working. The girls couldn't agree on their first store.

"Look, let's go in here first." Clover goes to the boutique where the men stood in groups.

"Why are we going to this store Clover? There is everything I want and very little I need in here."

"Exactly." Clover prances through the crowd of guys like she owned the boutique and behind her follows a timorous Chloe.

"Hey Chloe." Chloe turns back and flashes her icy white teeth.

"Hey Jeremy," she attempts to hide her smile, but her deep dimples give her away.

"What's up with you?" Clover butts in and answers.

"Not a damn thing."

"Aww, come on, don't be like Clover. What yawl been up to?"

"Just living, dodging fake niggas." Clover's sass was loud. She went into protection mode quick.

"Naw, it wasn't anything like that. I tried contacting Chloe like three or four times after that night but I couldn't get her. Lloyd said you had gotten back with your boyfriend." Clover was quick with lies and she wasn't going to let her sister go out like a chump, so she took it upon herself to delete Jeremy from the equation. Chloe stood confused until she notices the sneaky smirk on Clover's face.

"Oh yeah, we were trying to work things out." Clover darts her eyes at Chloe, *you go girl*, she thought.

"Oh okay. What are you doing later?" Clover crinkles her nose at Jeremy's pick-up line.

"No mister, you're going to have to come better than that," Clover jokes.

"Damn Clover, you're not going to give me no slack, are you?" Chloe covers her mouth as she giggles.

"Nope," Clover responds.

"Chloe can I take you out to eat later?" Hesitantly, Chloe answers, "I don't know, that depends. Are you going to sneak off with the waiter?" Chloe, Clover, and Jeremy all burst into laughter.

"Naw, I'm not going to do nothing like that."

"Cool, come by the house around eight- eight thirty." The girls continue their shopping. Boutique after boutique, they try on clothes in search of the perfect date fit, smelling fragrances and trying on shoes. The day was full of laughter, and for the first time in a while, Chloe was enjoying herself. Clover's plan was a success.

****

For as long as Chloe could remember, she's always been nervous: nervous about school, nervous about talking about men with her mother, and even more nervous to be alone with a man. Chloe's palms get sweaty and her knees begin to tremble as it comes time for her to deal with Jeremy on an intellectual and physical level. *Don't blow this Chloe, don't blow it*, she recites in her head as she feels Jeremy's stick harden on her buttocks.

"Did you enjoy dinner?" Chloe looks up into Jeremy's eyes; they were burning with passion. She knew he wanted her and he wanted her bad.

"Yeah it was nice; I mean we actually made it through this one without you skipping……" Jeremy places his finger over Chloe's full, juicy lips. For a reason she was unsure of, she was happy he did because she sure wasn't trying to ruin the moment. She attempts to tuck her fears away and grab control of her shattered nerves. She smiles at him, and then takes him by the hand and pulls him back into the hotel room she bought for the night.

"Are you sure you want to do this?" he asks before tossing her onto the hotel bed. Instead of answering Jeremy with words, Chloe takes his hand and places it between her legs. She was clothed in a baby-blue, leather skirt with a white bodysuit underneath and snow white silk panties. Chloe could feel Jeremy's fingers push the crotch of her body suit and panties aside and explore her wetness. It was better than she could ever imagine. Within the next ten minutes they were snatching each other's clothes off. Completely naked and out of her comfort zone, Chloe gives Jeremy the best night ever. She fucks him like she's a professional, although she's as fresh as fruit. The sex is so good, Jeremy has no idea she's a virgin. Her hormones were in control and her shyness was buried for the entire hour.

CHAPTER 16

The ride on the train to Georgia State was a joyous one. Chloe had been up all night pillow talking with Jeremy, and for the first time ever she felt alive and visible. She prances to the dormitories with no worries in tow. She was simply going to get the keys to her dorm, meet her roommate and be out. Since Chelsey promised her that she would help her move her things and get settled in on her off day.

Oh hell no, she thought as she opens her door and finds the mean girl from orientation unpacking her bag.

"Oh hey, I'm Latoya and I'll be your roommate. You must be Chloe?" Latoya's bright red lipstick and retro dress blend well with her bubbly personality.

"Yes, I'm Chloe." It was clear Latoya had no idea Chloe was the girl that she was super nasty to in the restroom just a week ago.

"Are you moving in today?" The large, ugly, blue-brown-yellow bruise catches Chloe's eye.

"No, not today, I'm going to wait until my mother is off so she can bring my things." As covertly as she could, Chloe looks at the bruise, then at Latoya's face. She seems smiley and happy, and otherwise a normal college student preparing for the semester.

"Did you want this side?"

"No, I don't have any preference." Chloe continues to check out the room but a few minutes later, something on Latoya's leg distracts her: yes it was another ugly looking, blue-brown-yellow bruise. Now it's hard for Chloe to focus. She looks at her face again and thinks about how normal she seems. For half of a second, Chloe considers saying something to Latoya about her bruises, but she didn't know what to say. So, she pretends to check out the closet space, awkwardly looking at the bruises on her leg and arm with a side-eye. *Is this girl going to be trouble? I think I might need to get my room changed. No chill Chloe, you don't know her story. She could be a klutz like you who walks into doorframes and tables and chairs with oblivion. She could be an actress and the bruises are just makeup. She could have leukemia. Or she could have at least two, ugly-looking visible bruises for some other good reason entirely.* Latoya's ringing cellular startles Chloe out of her daze.

"What do you want Lloyd?" Instantly, Chloe's ears grow attentive the conversation at the sound the name Lloyd.

"There is nothing you can say to me that will make things right. Did you see my face?" The seriousness in Latoya's voice was a new tone. Maybe she wasn't as good as she seem to be.

"You put your hands on me Lloyd. All because you got caught cheating." *Lord please let there be more than one Lloyd in Atlanta,* Chloe thought as she slides into the restroom to listen to Latoya's conversation in private.

"I can't believe you would do me like this, I just can't. You promised that you would never hit me again and to find out you've been cheating on me with this little young girl is just even more disgusting." Latoya's whimpers increase, and before she could get another word out, Chloe barges into the room and snatches the phone from her ear.

"Hello!" she speaks in a disguise voice.

"Who is this?" Chloe's heart drops to her gut as she recognizes Lloyd's voice on the other end of the phone.

"This is Latoya's roommate and I have to use the phone, so she's going to have to call you back." Before Lloyd could respond, Chloe ends the call.

"Thank you girl." If only Latoya knew that Chloe's actions wasn't for her benefit, she wouldn't be thanking her.

"Anytime girl, don't ever let him see you sweat. That's when he knows he got the best of you." Latoya nods in agreeance, wiping her bruised eye with a handkerchief.

"This isn't the first time he's hit you, is it?" Chloe shakes her head in shame as Latoya shakes her head *no*.

"You got to get out. How long have yawl been together?"

"For about three years now. I mean, it wasn't always like this. I remember the days he actually cared, took pride in flaunting me around, actually made it his business to make me smile. But as of six months to a year ago, things just changes. He's constantly yelling and angry about something. It's like the only way he's happy is when he's hitting me." Chloe was surprised to see Latoya, who seemed so confident just a couple of days ago, open up to someone like her. I mean she had no shame. She was spilling the tea, freely.

"I think we're going to work out just fine Chloe." *I don't know about that,* Chloe thought.

"Yeah, I think we are too. So, tell me something, do I need to get a Taser, some pepper spray and extra locks?"

"No, you're fine. He's not that kind of psycho."

"Okay, good. So he doesn't go to Georgia State?"

"No, he attends GS but he's not stupid enough to come to my dorm with that craziness. He only becomes a wolf behind closed doors." *He attends GS, that bastard said he went to Georgia Tech.* Chloe grew livid as she put the pieces together silently in her head.

"Oh, so he's a coward type?"

"Exactly." Chloe wrestles through her purse to find her ringing phone.

"I have to take this, but I'll be here bright and early tomorrow with my things." She speaks before anxiously running out the room to give Chelsey the tea.

"Okay girl, I'll see you soon."

"You wouldn't believe my day," Chloe answers.

"Well hello to you too."

"I'm sorry, hello momma. How was your day?"

"It was okay."

"That's good; now let me tell you about mine." Chelsey giggles at Chloe's lack of care for her day.

"What's been going on with you honey? I'm all ears."

"Well for starters, I was blessed with the professor from hell. I mean this man has no good reviews and everybody that speaks about him around campus says he's the absolute worse. So yea, I'm going to have a challenging first semester." Chelsey continues to giggle at Chloe's dramatics.

"Oh yeah, and I met your daughter's boyfriend's girlfriend."

"What?" Instantly, Chelsey's tone changes.

"Where... how... what you mean?"

"Oh she's just my roommate," Chloe sasses. "The girl was crying and bruised and apparently he did it because she found out about Clover."

"Oh my goodness!" Chelsey blurts. "How do you know that it's Clover's Lloyd?"

"Because I snatched the phone and pretended like I was basically her friend, of course I disguised my voice, but it was definitely him." Chloe smacks like the gum is too good, only she doesn't have gum in her mouth, just a juicy story.

"Oh my goodness, make sure you break it to her gently Chloe."

"Oh I'm not telling her, that's your job," Chloe snaps.

"She's your sister, Chloe."

"She's your daughter, Chelsey."

"If I tell her, she will know we were discussing it." Chloe remembers how bad she felt when she believed Clover and Chelsey were discussing her behind her back.

"Okay, well, we can tell her together."

"Cool, I'll wait 'til you get home."

Chapter 17

There's no discounting the importance of the first day of class. What happens that day sets the tone for the rest of the course and Chloe wasn't setting a good tone. As she stumbles into class twelve minutes after the hour she's expected to arrive, the class watches attentively. One pencil, one phone, and then a handful of books scatter onto the floor.

"Whenever you're ready, we can start class Ms...?" Chloe clumsily looks up and answers, "Chloe, Chloe Winter." For a long second, Professor Banks pauses with his mouth drooped open.

"Dang Professor Banks, she not on "America's Most Wanted," is she?" His stoned face was obvious and the kids didn't mind taking turns shooting jokes.

"It's probably his long lost daughter," one student blurts.

"Whenever you're ready Chloe Winter, we can start class. And Antonio, the class has you to thank for their first twenty-page paper."

"Mannnn," the class sang in unison.

"I told you, this is going to be a long semester," the thick sister whispered to the nerdy Asian girl next to her.

"A long semester it will be, so get comfortable Ms. White." *Shit, he must have elephant ears*, Tameka White thought.

What is a good writer? Professor Banks turns to the board and vividly writes in large print.

"Someone who can bring out an emotion in readers!" Chow, the Chinese boy yells out.

"A good writer can be anyone with a great imagination," Chloe's neighbor, Stephanie, answers before looking over at the racket noise she was making. Chloe could barely get settled. Her things were steadily slipping from her hand and her desk was sliding with her every movement.

"How about you Chloe Winter, what is a good writer to you?" Nervously, she looks up to answer Professor Banks.

"A good writer to me is a writer......" *I want you to make me feel like I'm the only girl in the world, like I'm the only one that you'll ever love.*

"I'm sorry, just give me one minute!" Chloe blurts, wildly scuffling through her purse for her phone.

"Ooh the index finger, I guess we're on her time Professor Banks." The class chuckles at Johnny, the class clown.

"Momma, I can't talk right now, I'm in class. Bye Chelsey."

"Okay, I'm sorry. Now what was I saying? Oh yeah…" Cut off in the middle of her thought, the Professor interrupts her answer and continues with his lecture.

"Class your first assignment is to write me a great story. Fiction, memoir, non-fiction, scientific, whatever floats your boat. I need to know who my writers are and who's here to waste my time. The weak stories will not only get an *F but* get thrown out of my class."

The class sighs in harmony, looking around at each other as if it may be the last time they all sit together in one class.

"This is an honors class, meaning it is a privilege for you to be here. Now earn your stay. Papers are due on Thursday; now go make your parents proud." The class rounds up their things as the bell dismisses them.

"Chloe Winter, I'd like to have a word with you." *Shit, I'm already fucked. Shit, shit, damn!* She thought as she made her way to Professor Banks' desk.

"I'm sorry about everything, it'll never happen again. Today has just been very hectic for me." David listened with an expressionless face. He truly didn't care about her disrupting the class; he was just relieved that she hadn't noticed who he was. Chloe was seven the last time she saw him and clearly her memory wasn't knowledgeable of his identity.

"I know it'll never happen again because if it does, you're out of my class. Do I make myself clear?" noisily, Chloe swallows her saliva and nods in agreeance. Right after, Chelsey burns Chloe's line again.

"And tell your mother, stopping being a nag and worry ball." Chloe wrinkles her forehead with confusion. *Man he called her out, right on the money*, she thought before picking up the phone.

CHAPTER 18

"Thanks momma." Chloe goes to the library with her phone pasted to ear and her bags sloppy thrown across her shoulder. She was truly a clumsy geek walking.

"Oh, what did I do to deserve that?" Chelsey jokes as she catches the sarcasm in Chloe's voice.

"You just helped me make an enemy with the world's meanest Professor, Professor Banks." Instantly, Chelsey's heart drops to her stomach and her words gets caught up in her throat. She's silent for about a minute or two, while Chloe continues to ramble.

"First, I come in super late and as if that wasn't enough, I disrupt the class with my clumsiness. There goes my new school boo down the drain."

"Why do you need a school boo anyway? I thought you and Jeremy were hitting off?" Chelsey finally snaps back to reality and asks.

"We are but it's always good to have back up momma."

"I guess you're right. Um, where did you say your Professor was from again?" Chelsey wanted to be sure that her speculations were right.

"He's from New York, anyway, I think he might kick me out, so it doesn't even matter." *There can't be that many Professor Banks' from New York teaching literature.* Chelsey thought as she put the pieces together to the puzzle.

"Oh yeah, he told me to tell you to stop nagging and to stop being such a worry ball. Isn't that weird? He got you down to the "t" and he doesn't even know you." Chloe giggles while Chelsey panics. *What the hell is David doing in Atlanta? And why hasn't he told me he's living here now?* Chelsey's thoughts were on go.

"Momma, will you come up here and talk to him for me?" Chelsey couldn't hear Chloe's question over her loud thoughts. *Shit, I'm glad he had his name changed. The last thing I need is the girls questioning me about him.*

Chelsey was almost positive her ex-husband was Chloe's new professor. He had always called her a worry-ball. Those were his exact words whenever she'd worry too much. Plus, David changed his name from his mother's name, Winter, to his father's name Banks. It was part of his exercise in the twelve step program. A new identity was supposed to make them feel like a new person.

"Momma, don't you hear me talking to you?" Chloe's loud outburst finally snaps Chelsey out her daze.

"I'm sorry, what you say baby?"

"I said can you come up…." Taken by surprise, Chloe's eyes locks with Jeremy. There he stood in Georgia State's library, cuddled up with a bubbly blonde. Chloe could hardly breathe; she felt butterflies dancing on her intestines.

"What were you asking me baby?" Speechless, Chloe ends the call with Chelsey and then dashes out of the library. On her way out, she trips over her own feet, bringing unwanted attention to her. The gut-wrenching horror of running into Jeremy on a date with another woman was now reality, only she didn't expect it to be in her school, since Jeremy had never mentioned during their many late-night conversations that he would be attending GS.

"Shit, fuck!" she murmurs before running into what seemed to be a supply closet.

"How could you be so stupid Chloe?" she blurts before bursting into sobbing. The humiliation was shocking and the pain was intense. It felt like knives stabbing her in the gut. Tightly, she grips onto her stomach and slides her back down the door until her buttocks is resting on the floor and her head is resting on her knees.

"I hate him, I hate him," she weeps. Her blood boils, turning her body hot to cold, cold to hot.

"Ms. Winter, are you okay?" Startled, Chloe jumps up at the sound of Professor Banks' voice. Caught in her feelings, she hadn't paid any attention to her surroundings. Four different teachers watched as she cried her heart out on the floor. Shit, this is the *teachers' lounge*, she thought.

"Yes, I'm okay," she answers before running out of the room, dropping her manuscript behind.

CHAPTER 19

Nervously, Chelsey sprinkles a large amount of Cayenne pepper onto her chicken breast. She had hesitated on filling Jessica in on the news all night and finally, she was ready to spill the tea.

"So guess whose back in town?" With a mouth full of soup, Jessica slurps down her dinner and then answers.

"I already know, I was wondering when you were going to find out."

"Oh my goodness, you mean to tell me you knew all this time and you're just now saying something?" Unbothered, Jessica grubs on her toast.

"I mean, I really don't feel like it's any of our business who Aunt Maggie takes into her home. If she is cool with the little thief living under her roof, then so am I. I'm no longer putting my nose where it doesn't belong." Relieved, Chelsey heavily exhales.

"Are you telling me Aunt Maggie let Samantha back into her house after all that drama?" Confused, quickly Jessica retorts.

"Yeah, who did you think I was speaking about?"

"Well honestly speaking, I thought you were talking about David."

"David? David Winter, your husband David!" Guests at nearby tables swivel their necks to fixate on Jessica.

"Damn loud mouth, tell everybody," Chelsey whispers, taking another sip of her margarita.

"Oh I'm sorry, my bad. I was loud, ugh?"

"Yes, anyway. David is back in town. He's no longer going by David Winter but David Banks."

"Wait, isn't that his daddy's name?"

"Yeah, he had to get a new name for his twelve step program. A new name equals a new person minus the old habits." Jessica frowns like she inhaled the worst smell.

"I commend him for trying, I really do, because he is one sick bastard."

"Jessica!"

"Okay, I mean; he's not normal. How about that?" Jessica was a handful and her mouth was loaded with bullets Chelsey didn't want to get shot with, so she just shook her head.

"How long has he been here?" Jessica asks.

"That's the thing, I don't know. I believe he's been here for a while because he has a job and everything."

"A job, where? I hope not around children honey."

"Jessica stop it."

"What, I'm just saying Chelsey, he doesn't need to be around children with his addiction."

"He's working over at Georgia State University."

"Oh, okay, that's cool. He's not in to adults." Heavily, Chelsey exhales with frustration.

"Okay calm down, I'm sorry."

"I'm just mad he didn't bother to tell me he was in town. I mean that's the least he could have done."

"I mean why does it matter Chelsey? Yawl are not together anymore; he's moved on and you've moved on." Chelsey's silence catches Jessica attention.

"You have moved on, right?" The dinner table is silent for twenty long seconds.

"Oh my goodness Chelsey, come on!" Instantly, after Jessica's comment, Chelsey bursts into laughter.

"That'll teach your ass to stop playing with me."

"Girl, you almost gave me a heart attack."

"What happened to, 'I'm not sticking my nose in nobody's business?' It sure seems like your nose is in mine." Jessica chuckles all while sipping on her mixed drink.

"Oh you weren't included in that package," she jokes.

"Anyway, the bill is on you."

"No it's not chic. You're the one who gets alimony, not me," Jessica jokes.

****

Yellow, polka dot, red, cotton bandage, silk; some of Chelsey's best dresses were laid out on her bed. She and David had a ugly past and he did some things she probably would never be able to fully forgive him for but that didn't change the fact, she wanted to sweat when he seen her.

She had tried on most of the dresses and still couldn't pick one. She searches for a special one to cover her curves when she accidentally bumps into David.

"Oh hey, what are you doing here?" she rehearses in the mirror.

"Nope, that doesn't seem real. David, is that you? Oh hey, Mr. Banks. Hey, you're living in Atlanta now? Shoot, who am I kidding? I bet he already assumes I know he's here. I should just go up there and tell him we need to talk, fuck the bullshit." Cool wind from Chelsey's deep exhale blows her thinning Chinese bang upward. She flops her butt down onto her queen-sized mattress, disappointed. She couldn't get right. She contemplates for thirty minutes about approaching David or not while staring at an old picture of them on the nightstand.

"Man, why did I have to love this man so much?" she murmurs before her eyes lock on her and David's sex tape. It was stashed behind her freak-um dresses and now that she had moved them, there the tape was. For months Chelsey had been tearing her room up looking for her and David's tapes. Quickly, she runs into the closet and snatches them up. Originally, she searched for the tapes to get rid of them because she couldn't stomach the girls getting ahold of them, but now, she was eager to watch them, all ten of them. So she did, Chelsey masturbated off five of the ten tapes her and David made before drifting off to sleep.

CHAPTER 20

Oil sheen, perfume and body lotion scent the room as both Chloe and Latoya get ready for class. It had been two long days of funk for Chloe and she was finally ready to face the world again. For a minute, she contemplated on whether she should save face and purposely write a weak paper, but then she thought about that *F* that would follow her right out of his class.

"Why are you going to class so early? I thought we were going to grab a bite to eat and catch up on girl talk?" *Correction, you mean catch up on your work*, Chloe thought as she slid on her Converse.

"No, I have something I need to do before I go to class, so I'm going to have to take a rain check."

Chloe could tell from Latoya's facial expression that she was mad. She had high hopes on Chloe helping her with her paper like last time.

"Okay that's fine," she lies.

"I swear you look too young to be in college, are you sure you're over eighteen or are you one of those child geniuses?" Latoya jokes before jetting out.

"Yes, I'm grown; I just don't wear the tightest thing in my closest like you," Chloe murmurs after Latoya is gone.

****

"Come on in Ms. Winter," Professor Banks' voice startles Chloe. She assumed he couldn't hear her creeping into the class.

"I've been waiting on you." *You have, why?* Chloe thought as she slowly approaches his desk.

"Well, I guess we've been looking for each other." Chloe clears the static in her voice; she only wanted to apologize once. So it was best she made her words clear the first time around.

"I'm here to say, I'm sorry for my behavior in your class and out. It was wrong of me and…Well; usually I'm never like this but…"

"Really?" Professor Banks chuckles.

"No really, I'm never really this unstable. I'm usually a good student who has her stuff together but for some reason this year, I've been thrown off my game, but don't worry, I'm getting it together."

"You've been thrown off your game or a boy has thrown you off your game, which one?" *Shit, why does it always have to be a boy? I mean it's true, but damn, there could be other things that throw girls off their game.*

"A little bit of both to be honest." David pulls his glasses off his face and then finally for the first time looks into Chloe's beautiful brown eyes. For ten long, awkward seconds they stare into one another's eyes.

"Never apologize for things that are out of your control and tears from a broken heart, are usually out of your control." The sparkle from Chloe's eyes blend with her natural glow. *Damn, was it that obvious I was crying over a boy? Shit, they probably all sat in the lounge talking about me and shit.*

"You got a good thing going here. I like to feel a lot more emotion and I'd love for you to paint better scenery, but the story is good." Stunned, Chloe slowly grabs her manuscript from Professor Banks.

"Oh my goodness, you read my story?"

"Well, yes and I think you'll have a guaranteed seat here in this class if you turn in this story for your assignment."

"This was a private journal Professor Banks; you had no right."

"Well, maybe next time you'll be careful where you leave your prized possessions, now won't you?" *Touché,* she thought.

"If you like, I can give you some private tutorial lessons. I see potential in you and I'd like to help you get to where you're going, but you'll have to get permission from your mother." *My mother's permission? I'm grown.*

"With all due respect Professor Banks, this is college not high school. I'm grown; I don't need my mother's permission to get tutoring. However, I am a little curious as to why you would help me after I've been so disruptive in your class." Professor Banks snatches off his tan Kangaroo hat and pushes his fine hair back.

"Take a good look at me Chloe and tell me what you see?" Confused for a long twenty seconds, Chloe shakes her head searching for the missing clue to the mystery puzzle.

"I'm really not sure what I should be looking for, can you be a little more specific?" After giggling for five seconds, David responds.

"I'm the original owner of that name you carry." *I'm the original owner of that name your carry, I'm the original owner of that name your carry,* Chloe recites David's hint in her head until a light bulb lights up.

"Oh my goodness! David, is that you?"

"Yes Chloe." Chloe's face shines like a diamond.

"So like I was saying, get your mother's permission and then we can talk about the tutoring." The classroom begins to pile up, so Chloe quickly answers.

"Okay, I'll set up dinner. It'll be a great. All of us at one table again. Come to the house around eight tomorrow," she whispers before taking her seat.

CHAPTER 21

"I will not hug him. I will not smell him and I will not look him in the eye." Chelsey murmurs as she perfects herself in the mirror.

"Will you get out the mirror already?" Watching Chelsey obsess over her look begin to bug Chloe out. She hated when Chelsey and Clover obsessed over their appearance because to her, they were perfect. Even at forty-plus Chloe felt her mother still outshines her. She stands five foot seven, is curvy and has a face cut right from the pages of a men's magazine. Chloe, on the other hand, had stopped growing at five foot four inches, and she had the sort of face people confused with a kid even after she'd loaded layers of makeup.

"Chelsey, you look beautiful. Now can you come on, so we can eat already?" Chelsey took one last spin in the mirror, added another layer of her favorite Ruby-Woo red lipstick and then tucked in her stomach.

"Okay, I'm ready, let's go eat," she said as she followed Chloe out the room.

"Wow, momma, you look great!" Clover announced as Chelsey made her way down to the seating area. The clicking of her heels added rhythm to the soft classical music David loved to listen to back in the day. Her eyes curiously scanned the room but there was no David, just Clover and her big smile.

"I've never seen you look this stunning before," Clover said.

"I know right? She cleans up nice for an old witch," Chloe jokes.

"So where is this lucky fella, he didn't get scared, did he?" Chelsey's body tenses up, the thought of being stood up by David shook her nerves.

"I don't know where Chloe's guest is but I'm ready to eat, so let's eat," Chelsey snapped.

"He'll be here, he'll be here. Just give him a minute," Chloe said.

"Well, we're not about to wait on him. He can just join us when he gets here. I'm about to eat," Clover retorted before making herself comfortable at the dinner table.

"You're so greedy Clover." As soon as Chloe takes her seat at the table the doorbell rings.

"The last person standing, gets the door!" Chloe yells out to Chelsey.

"I don't know how I let yawl set me up to be the host of this little shindig," Chelsey mumbles on her way to the door. "I'm coming, I'm coming!" David repeatedly rings the doorbell to rattle Chelsey's nerves.

"If you ring this doorbell one more time," Chelsey blurts before slinging the door open.

David steps from the shadows, stealing Chelsey's breath and the heat from her skin. Suddenly, her defenses are just paper; paper that is being soaked by the rapidly falling salty teardrops. Before she can draw in the air her body needs she melts into his arms. She can feel his firm torso and the heart that beats within. His hands are folded around her back, drawing her in closer.

"You're aging like wine Chelsey." Chelsey can feel her body shake, crying for the missed time they will never make back, crying to release the tension of the bold anger she held inside for so long.

"Don't cry beautiful." He pulls is head back and wipes the tears with his soft finger. David is eating Chelsey with his eyes, running his hand through her hair, as if he can't quite believe she's not part of an almost forgotten dream. Slowly, David leans in for a big one. When he kisses Chelsey it's sweet, gentle, and it tastes of her tears. She wants to speak but all she can do is croak, "I'm happy to see you David, it's been a long time." His mouth paints a soft smile and he nods once before folding her into his arms again.

"Yes, it has."

"Yawl do know food don't stay warm for nobody, right?" Chloe chuckled at Clover's joke.

"Wow, Clover you've gotten so big girl. How is life treating you?"

"Oh, you know. Terrible." In unison, they all laughed.

"Hang in there, it gets worse." He jokes. Chelsey was taken back by David's gentlemanly ways. It had been a minute since a man pulled a chair out for her.

"Yeah, about that college thing," Clover blurts as David finally takes his seat.

"Yeah, what about it?"

"Well, I was thinking I could use my college fund to invest in my business."

"You still need college to start a business, Clover. Entrepreneurship is not as easy as it may seem." Chelsey was happy to have David around to help her get through to Clover.

"So what's this business you're trying to start?" Quickly, Clover switches the channel.

"Enough about me, what are doing here out of the blue? I thought you were like in New York or something like that." The cool wind from Chloe's mouth blew her bang upward as she exhaled irritably. She could feel the drama coming and she didn't need anything to get in the way of David's decision to help her write.

"Clover, I swear you're the rudest, most ungrateful person I know."

"Dang, calm down! It's not that serious Chloe!" Clover snapped before stuffing her mouth with the loaded potatoes.

"No, it's a good question Chloe. I would also like to know how long you've been back in Atlanta David." David could feel everyone's eyes burning a hole right through his skin. The heat was on but he wasn't surprised. He took his time to chew and swallow his steak and if that didn't make them wait long enough, David took even more time to wash down his food with the southern style sweet tea.

"As you girls know, I didn't leave on a good tip. So, I assumed it would be better if I just let you ladies live in peace. I just didn't want to impose and cause more drama Chelsey. That's all."

"Yeah, whatever happened with yawl anyway? Did you cheat or something?" Clover questioned.

"Oh my goodness, Clover!"

"What? Why you got your panties in a bunch? Don't you want to know too?"

"That's something your mother would have to explain to you girls." Chelsey was eating her dinner like she thought it was poisoned. Each forkful was tinier than what you'd feed a baby, and even then, she nibbled it. She had no appetite and she was trying her best to hide her emotions. She heard David, but her heart didn't. She'd always dreamed that he would come back to her with his shit together, begging to make things right.

"Even before we were married, we were friends. I just feel like you abandoned me at my most trying moment in life. Excuse me if I can't forgive you for your selfishness." A web of tears form in the corner of Chelsey's eyes as she croaks out her feelings.

"A phone call, a descent visit anything would have been nice David. Anything!" Speechless, David just watched as Chelsey spilled her guts.

"So, are you remarried?" Chelsey asks.

"No, I promised myself I wouldn't marry another woman after you. You were too good to me Chelsey and I know that and I wish sorry was enough but I know better. It'll never be enough. That's why I don't come around." Chelsey could feel her heart leave her body when David rises from the table. She didn't want to lose him again, but she couldn't find the words to make him stay.

"I'm sorry for ruining everyone's dinner. Chelsey, I wish you the best and I pray you find the kind of love that will make you glow like the disco ball." Chelsey remembered that corny joke. It was a joke David would use when he wanted to butter Chelsey for something he wanted, but not even her favorite joke could bring her to a smile. Things weren't going her way and she didn't know how to grab control.

"You don't have to leave!" Chloe blurted out Chelsey's feelings.

"No, I think it's best I do. Good luck on that business Clover." Chelsey's tears slowly drip from her chin. She didn't even bother to wipe them because they were consistently running.

"David wait!" Chloe yelled as she ran out the house behind him.

"Does this mean you're not going to help me with my writing?" Chloe knew her question was selfish at a time like this but she didn't care.

"Yes. If you want me to, I'll still help you with your writing Chloe."

"Yes," Chloe whispers. "Thank you David, thank you so much!" As David disappeared out the driveway, an unknown vehicle was pulling up. Chloe's smile quickly turned into a frown when she noticed Lloyd was the stranger getting out of the car.

"What the hell are you doing here?" Lost for words, Lloyd didn't know what to say.

He stuttered, "Oh, I'm here for Clover. She invited me for dinner. Am I too late?"

"No baby, you're not too late. Come on in, don't mind my sister. She's just a little over protective!" Clover yelled from the porch.

"You just don't care what stray you take in, do you? I hope you know this dog is already taken!" Chloe, was thirty-eight hot about how the night had taken off but she was happy that David still agreed to help her with her writing.

"Don't mind her baby, she's just a bitter old woman trapped in a little girl's body." Lloyd tried to hold in his laughter but he failed miserably. Clover would never know how her joke cut Chloe. She was already struggling with her self-esteem and Clover wasn't making matters any better. Quickly, Chloe dashed through the house and upstairs to her room. She couldn't stomach Lloyd seeing her cry.

"Sister, where are you going?"

"Fuck you Clover!" Chloe yelled from the top of the staircase and then slammed her room door.

"What a dinner," Clover murmured.

CHAPTER 22

Mesmerized by the view, Chloe pulls up slow to the cabin. Ivy and ferns grew through the crevices of the old winding stone path, which led her directly to the colossal cottage. The cabin emerged proudly behind creaky wooden fences, edged by rows of skeletal trees crowned in crimson, swaying gently to the chilly autumn wind.

Wow, this is beautiful, Chloe thought as she put the car in park. "Oh my goodness." Silently, David watches as Chloe appreciates nature's beauty. A deep sense of serenity overcomes her as she stares in rapture at the expanse of blue that lay before her. Rays of light danced delicately across the lake, birthed from the afternoon sun that both limited her sight and made the view even more beautiful.

"I asked you to meet here because….."

"Because it's writing heaven," Chloe blurts finishing David sentence.

"Well come on in, let me show you around." Like Dorothy, Chloe skipped on up the stone path with her laptop in tow.

"How were the directions?"

"Oh, the directions were fine but I thought I would never get here."

"Yeah, the ride seems long when you don't know where you're going, but once you've made the ride about four times, it doesn't even bother you."

"I'm sure you've written some masterpieces out here."

"The view definitely helps get the juices flowing. Hopefully, it'll get your rhythm flowing because from what I've read, you don't have no rhythm," David jokes.

"I beg your pardon," Chloe retorts.

"I'm sorry, but the dancing scene in this story had me cringing." Amused, David could barely breathe from all the laughter.

"Oh, you wrong for that." Just as soon as Chloe flops down into the sofa, David pulls her back up.

"No ma'am, this music is for you."

"Oh is it? I thought maybe I was interrupting your groove." Sweet Jazz hummed from the old record player.

"The best writers pull from true life experiences. I'm assuming you're not the best dancer and it shows in your writing. You need to know how it actually feels to two-step with a man."

Chloe chuckles and retorts, "Yeah, only I don't think you should use the phrase two-step anymore. It just kills the mood." For a split second, David joins Chloe in laughter and then like an entertaining clown his body begins to move.

The music was like liquid adrenaline being injected right into his blood stream. He'd never had a dance class, but he and Chelsey had jived to music since their early twenties, competing in the friendly way couples do to "up" one another.

"Oh I see you don't need to warm up or nothing, do you?" Chloe watches in amusement. David moves around good for a man playing of fifty. He was like a well-oiled machine on the dance floor and she could tell he wasn't the show off type, which made his moves appear even more smooth.

"Feel free to join in when you're ready." Chloe wasn't sure if she wanted to dance with someone whose limbs were half liquid; in perfect rhythm.

"Come on, don't be scared. This is a no judgement zone." After battling back and forth with her timid alter ego, Chloe finally decided to join David. He could tell she wasn't a mover and shaker, kinda shy in the way she moved, but he saw determination in her efforts. He wanted to compliment her on her courage but for the first time in years, he felt like if he opened his mouth nothing witty or interesting would come out.

Chloe looks up and the two lock eyes. For obvious reasons, David pulls away from the dance. The chemistry was becoming embarrassing for the both.

"Well, I don't think you need me anymore. You got the idea. I can't teach you how to write, you got to let life lead you with that. But I can help you perfect what you've already written once you've pieced it together. So, here's the key to the cabin. Feel free to use it as much as you like. I'm barely here anymore anyway."

"So that's it, you're just going to leave me alone?"

"Yes, you'll find being along helps the process tremendously. Don't worry, nobody will get you, you're safe here. If you get spooked, call me or use the handgun in the bedroom closet."

"Wait, David!" Chloe speeds out the house behind David.

"Yes?" he turns and answers.

"Whatever happened to you and Chelsey?"

"You have to let her talk to you about that Chloe. It's not my place."

"Well, I just wanted to let you know I wasn't mad at you for leaving. I mean whatever it was, it's in the past now and shit. Everybody deserves second chances." David didn't bother responding. He jumped into his Jeep wrangler and disappeared into nature's beauty.

CHAPTER 23

"Whose pussy this is? Let me hear you say it."

"It's yours's daddy, it's yours!" Kelly heard a group of girls' giggling voices echoing down the hall, but she assumes she and Lloyd are safe since Chloe was away at some cabin to write.

"Baby we have to stop before someone figure us out." Lloyd ignores Kelly's plea and continues to pound away at her box. He wasn't stopping until he got his nut for the day. He fucked her without mercy. The girls could hear the sound of his balls slamming up against Kelly's ass. They all listened outside the door at her screaming for mercy. The louder the *oohing* and *aahhing* got, the more the crowd increased. Quickly, Chloe brushed through the crowd when she noticed it was her dorm everyone was surrounding.

"Excuse me, excuse me. Let me through dammit!" forcefully, Chloe pushed open the door.

"What the fuck is going on in here? Are fucking kidding me right now!" Quickly, Lloyd jumps up from the bed dressing swiftly like he had just been caught doing Kelly by her father. The sight of his dick with veins bulging from all direction triggers Chloe's frustration and before he could get his penis zipped in his pants good, Chloe charges him with all her might. He manages to block his face from the punches with his forearm but not his penis.

"You nasty muthafucker! You don't ever come back around my sister again! You creep, you fuckin' loser!" Unstoppable, Chloe goes bat-shit crazy on Lloyd; punching, slapping and kicking. She was beyond furious and was determined to collect revenge for her sister.

"Yo, Kelly get this bitch off me!" Silently, Kelly stood off in the corner confused by Chloe's rage.

"You want some of this shit bitch?" Quickly, Kelly dashed to the corner. She was in no shape to take on the monster. The snake like veins swiveling on Chloe's forehead were horrific.

"Chloe, what is your problem? Calm down! What's wrong?"

"What's wrong is you're fucking the same dirty dog my sister is fucking. Then you're all fucking loud and shit. The whole freaking dorm could hear you. You just don't have no respect for yourself." Kelly knew better than to argue with Chloe, her emotions were too high.

"Okay, you're yelling at me like I knew that Chloe!" Swiftly, Lloyd jetted out the door while Chloe and Kelly threw words at one another.

"You didn't have to know that to have respect for yourself. You got the whole fucking dorm listening to you fuck this slum dog ass nigga."

"So, hold up, back up for a second. You mean to tell me that you knew all this long time that your sister was fucking my man?"

"I just found out when the slum nigga came to my house for dinner." It took everything in Kelly to fight back her tears. The day had easily turned into the worse day ever.

"What the fuck yawl looking at?" Chloe yells out to the giggling girls in the hallway. Afterwards, she looks back at Kelly. The laughter was obviously getting to her. Shamefully, Kelly dresses herself with her head held low. Tears begin to build up in the web of her eyes but she refuses let them drop. Chloe thought about comforting her and maybe even apologizing for her awful behavior but she didn't. Instead, she dashed out the dorm with her books and bag in tow.

****

After three drinks and a meal, Chloe finally arrives at Chelsey's house. Night has fallen and enveloped the city in a blanket of darkness. She drags down the path towards the house, her shoes slapping against the stone steps that lead to the front door.

"Clover, I got some bad news for you." Fallen leaves litter the walkway, bathing it in dark red and orange, and Chloe steps on them just to hear the satisfying crunch. She was a drink away from drunk.

"Clover, Chelsey, open the door!" The porch light was on, so Chloe assumes that Chelsey and Clover are sitting in the living area. Straddling for her balance, the drinks were slowly settling in. Chloe drops her books and bag on the porch and then digs in the brand-new flower pot to the right of the door that's filled with pink and yellow chrysanthemums for the spare key.

"So, nobody wants to let me in, huh?" Chloe murmurs. The metal of the doorknob is cool against her palm as she twists it with ease, entering the well-lit living room as if she's the awaited surprise.

"I'm home!" she yells out to the empty room.

"Chelsey, Clover, where are you? Chelsey, are you home?" Slowly, Chloe wobbles her way up the stairs to Chelsey's room, but to her surprise there was no Chelsey, just a floor full of VHS tapes. Carelessly, she flops onto the floor to do the obvious; be nosey.

"So what do we have here?" she mumbles before popping one of the tapes into the VCR.

"You should have never disobeyed daddy, now you're going to get it."

Chloe couldn't believe her eyes. Her palms grew sweaty and butterflies begin to swim in her guts, but she didn't turn off the cassette.

"I'm sorry baby, I never meant to disobey you..." Chelsey moans out just before David yanks her by her schoolgirl ponytails.

"It's too late to apologize now, lay down."

David had a deep, mesmerizing, sexy-ass voice, to Chloe and she couldn't believe that he and Chelsey's little freak show was turning her on. During her high school days, she would get grossed out hearing Chelsey and Jessica share their sex stories but seeing things in action had a different impact. David is looking more like a snack than her step dad and she barely pays attention to Chelsey. So it didn't feel like she was watching her mom. Chloe leans her back up against the corner of the bed with her eyes glued to the plasma.

"Ohhhhh, daddy!"

It was dead quiet throughout the house and Chelsey's loud *ooooing* and *ahhhing* had Chloe's heartbeat increasing like a kid stealing candy.

"I need to hear you say it," David groans out as he pounds away at Chelsey's cakes.

"I'm sorry daddy, I'll never disobey you again." Without notice Chloe props open her legs and begin to massage clitoris. The more Chelsey moans and begs David to stop, the faster Chloe massages her clit. She was tired of being sexless and her body was yearning to be touched. She shoves two of her fingers into her vagina and thrust them in and out, in and out.

"Momma, you did not have to do that man like that, oh my goodness." The loud giggling and snickering from the hallway startles Chloe and quickly she jumps up and stops the tape. Before Chelsey walks in the room, Chloe meets her in the hall.

"Where have yawl been?" Frightened by Chloe's presence, both Chelsey and Clover jump and screams.

"Aaah! Girl where did you come from?"

"I just got here. Clover, I need to talk to you."

CHAPTER 24

"Where yawl coming from, making all this noise?" Chloe's nerves were shattered. She'd be so embarrassed if Chelsey knew what she was doing.

"What you doing at home on a school day?" Chelsey tries to enter her room that Chloe has guarded but Chloe blocks her every attempt.

"No, I think you need to stay for this," Chloe says.

"Stay for what? What's going on Chloe?"

"Yeah, what do you have to tell me?"

Chloe takes a deep breath, rolls her eyes and retorts, "I know this is not something you want to hear but Lloyd is cheating on you. Well really, you're his side piece."

Arrogantly Clover giggles, "You right, I don't want to hear it Chloe. You're just a hater and you seriously need to get a life. I mean seriously, how long are you going to be this weird ass girl with no life?" Shouting rents the air. What was once peaceful becomes polluted with rage. Both Clover and Chloe are tense.

"You little fuckin' whore! I don't have to hate on you. You open your legs to anybody that shoots you a compliment. Excuse me for trying to tell you about the dog you call a man."

"Hold on now, you both need to just calm down and talk to each other like descent human beings at least. For God's sake, you're sisters." Once Chloe gets going there was no stopping her. She ignores Chelsey and continues her rant.

"I should have known you wouldn't care, you moral-less whore."

"You're the one to talk, you weird ass creep! You're just mad because no man wants to fuck you!"

"Watch your mouth Clover. Yawl not going to sit here and cuss like I'm not standing here." The shouting is a violence in the air and no one is listening, everybody is just screaming at one another.

"I'm virgin bitch because I don't just give it up to anybody." She lied. She wasn't a virgin anymore but it felt like it because she wasn't consistently having sex.

"Yeah, right. No one wants your ass Chloe." The pressure of her day is balled-up inside of Chloe like a tangled knot and she's a ticking bomb ready to explode. Clover's words were cutting Chloe more than she was leading on and she couldn't take it anymore.

"Well fuck you bitch, I don't care anymore. You want to be a little whore then be my guest. I'll never waste my breath telling you anything else."

"You don't know Lloyd Chloe, you just being the typical judging Chloe you always are."

"Bitch I saw him with my roommate with my own eyes. The two have been together for a while. He's a woman beater and an asshole." Chloe didn't just raise her voice; her muscles tense and she moves in close for maximum impact.

"Don't you hit her Chloe. I mean it dammit!" Chelsey blurts out while invading Chloe's space.

"I'm finished with you Chloe; I don't have time for this shit," Clover retorts before storming off into her room and slamming the door behind her.

"Chloe, have you been drinking or something?"

"Yes, but I'm not drunk. I was just trying to watch out for her. That's all." Without warning, tears pour from Chloe's eyes and she just breaks into sobbing.

"I'm sorry for disrespecting you momma, I don't know what's gotten into me lately."

"It's okay Chloe. I know you're just trying to look out for your sister, but there's a way to do everything. She's young and boy crazy. You can't just spring information on her like that. Stop crying, it's okay." Chelsey soothes Chloe with hugs and kisses.

Between sniffles, she asks Chelsey, "Momma can I ask you a question and you promise not to get mad?"

"Yes Chloe, what is it?"

"How do you feel about David? Are you still in love with him?"

"No, I don't love David anymore. What we had is history. Why Chloe? Where is all this coming from?" Slowly, the two kneel on the floor and tightly Chelsey wraps Chloe up in her arms, rocking her back and forth like a baby.

"I really want him to help me with my writing, but I don't want to do it without your permission." Instantly guilt showers Chelsey.

She never wants the girls to feel like they have to alter their life for her and even though she would prefer the girls stayed away from David, she wouldn't dare tell them to.

Softly, she wipes the snot running from Chloe's nose and answers, "Of course you have my permission Chloe. If you feel like he can help you, then take him up on his offer." Chelsey was willing to tell Chloe whatever she wanted to hear to keep the peace.

"Thank you momma. This really means a lot to me."

"You're welcome baby. Just don't forget about me when you blow up with your multiple *New York Times* Bestsellers."

"I won't, you have my word."

CHAPTER 25

For six hours straight Chloe's been sitting at the little round table with a white linen table cloth and burning candles. She's determined to finish up her book but sitting for the long hours makes her butt feel flatter than a week-old glass of coke. She glances over at the ticking clock on the wall and she swears it's slowing down. She's given herself ten hours to write. She wants to break but is afraid of the embarrassing thoughts that may resurface if she does. Every second she takes from writing; she spends it fantasizing about David.

She couldn't get his deep baritone voice out of her ear. She's been dreaming every night for two weeks straight that it was her David was chastising in the video instead of Chelsey. During class lectures she undresses him with her eyes and gets lost in daydreams about her milking his dick with her mouth.

"Uuh, I need some music. I got to dance." Chloe jumps up from the table as if something hot had fallen in her lap. She knew just sitting there would only make her think of David more and deadlines wait for no one.

"Let me make a little coffee, play a little music. That should wake me up," she mumbles to herself as she flips through David's music collection.

"Oh snap R Kelly, that should get the job done." Chloe slides across the floor with her arms in the air like the old school women would do when their jam came on.

"It's seems like you ready, girl are you ready to go all the way?" Turns out Chloe didn't need the coffee; R Kelly was getting the job done all by himself. She sings along with the music, arms waving from side-to-side above her head, head swaying and feet sliding. She's so in tune with the music she misses David's entrance. As soon as she makes her 360 turn, her eyes lock with his.

"Aaaaaah! Shit----Shoot!"

"I'm sorry, I didn't mean to scare you," David blurts with water dripping from his rain coat.

"How long have you been standing there?"

"Just a minute. I got your voicemail about you coming up here and I figured you didn't hear about the storm so I came to check on you." Embarrassed, Chloe rushes over to the stereo player.

"No, you don't have to turn it off. Keep dancing, you won't even notice I'm here."

"Cool, I'll keep the music on, but you're going to have to dance with me. You know, since you messed up my groove and all." Cockily, Chloe takes David by his wet hands and pulls him into the middle of the floor. The music brings them together as one.

Clumsily she squishes his foot under her own. Still he smiles brightly as their shoes click over the hardwood floor. He watches as her hair spins out and bounces more with each move and beat. *This is perfect*, Chloe thinks. It didn't matter if her moves were perfect, all that matter is how she feels. For once in her life she isn't the shy awkward girl. She feels confident and beautiful.

David wraps his chiseled muscles around her frame and Chloe has every intention of stopping him from getting too close until his hand touches her face. The acceleration of her heartrate has nothing to do with fear and everything to do with what her body wants. She looks away as if the outside world holds her attention, but after all this time he reads her like a book, his eyes on her chest, her breathing rate vividly increases. With a gentle finger, he reorients her face so that he holds the gaze she didn't want to give him, stealing the passion from her eyes in a way that only magnifies the spark.

One look into David's dark bedroom eyes and Chloe decides she doesn't care about the consequences or the circumstances, she wants him. She knew her body could not settle for another night's sleep without him. Slowly, she leans in for a kiss and there is no smile on his lips, only the hot intensity of his gaze that they both know is the start of the firestorm to come.

"I should go, I'm sorry." Embarrassed, David jerks away from Chloe and quickly grab his coat from the rack.

"Please don't go," she whispers.

"What?" David wasn't sure he was hearing right.

"You invade my every thought. I dream of you doing things to me all the time, whether I'm stuck in rush-hour traffic or listening to your lectures. The mere thought of you makes my juices flow." Stunned, David didn't know how to respond, so he didn't. He drops his coat and walks over to the sofa the throw blanket is sprawled across and lays it out on the floor by the fireplace.

"Come," he demands before laying down on top of the blanket. "Tell me what you fantasize about."

"Or, I can just show you." Slowly, Chloe kneels to David's level. He looks her in the eyes and says, "Chloe, I'm going to punish you for being so naughty." She runs her fingers across his cheeks and then take his hands and begins to suck on his fingers, putting each one entirely into her mouth and sucking it gently.

"Umm," her moans arouse David. Forcefully, he grabs her head and pulls her in closer and the kissing begins. Deeper and deeper, he's drawn into her as he continues to lick the innocence from her lips. His desire grows even more intense as her hands caress his back and the nape of his neck. After long minutes of kissing, he finally stands to rip his shirt off. Letting it fall silently to the floor.

"Come here." Gently, David massages Chloe's shoulders as he lowers the straps of her dress. Soon, the wonder of her exposed, hardened nipples and small breasts catches his eyes. Chloe pulls her arms from the straps and knowingly touches David where he needs to be touched the most, caressing his dick through the black slacks he's still wearing. She kisses him again with a passion full of fire. He cannot hold himself back any longer. He grabs her breasts and massage her tender nipples under his thumbs. With each stroke, he can feel his desire rising and so can she.

He reaches with an open mouth to take her itty-bitty breasts in. He licks the tip of her nipple just to taste the sweetness of her. He sucks her for a moment that seems to last for eternity. Then he bites gently into her tender fruit, pulling a little more with each increasing bite.

"Aww," she moans as the bites roughens. He stops for a moment, lifting his lips from her nipple. He then watches as her nipple shivers in the air. Chloe cannot take the tease any longer. Anxiously, she undoes his belt buckle and then unzips his pants. He helps her slide his pants and satin boxer shorts completely off, and then kicks them aside.

"I don't want to hear no crying, you hear me?"

"Yes daddy," Chloe answers, remembering that David liked to be in control. She looks at his beautiful, scrumptious-looking dick biting down on her bottom lip in anticipation. She's been sexless far too long and couldn't wait for whatever David had in store for her.

"Go ahead, grab him," David demands. Gently, she takes his penis into her hands and massages it up and down the shaft with one hand and caresses his balls lightly with the other. She wants so badly to partake in his splendid nectar. She takes the tip of her tongue and licks the head of his dick straight down the middle, immediately tasting his salty precum.

She wants some more, lots more, so she takes the head of his dick into her mouth and suckles on it, contracting her cheek muscles in and out as she attempts to draw every single drop of his precum that exists onto her awaiting taste buds.

"Aww, Chloe. Suck harder, longer, faster!" The intensity grows as David begin to feed Chloe like she's his trained dog. He glides more and more of his dick into her mouth each time he directs it in and out.

"Umm," she moans with delight as his dick fills her throat. Her own saliva begins to trickle out the sides of her mouth onto her erect nipples. She arches her neck so that she can deep-throat his entire dick. She can feel the head of it hitting up against her tonsils while his balls slam up against her chin. He tastes so delicious to her, it's almost scary. She knows for sure she's hooked because she doesn't want the night to end. After he cums all over her face, the two repeat the play all night. All weekend long David explores Chloe's body. Her kiddy-pie was heaven sent. She was his God sent angel and he was her knight and shining armor. They could care less about the outside world and who their actions might offend.

CHAPTER 26

The perfumed, air conditioned mall is heaven to Chelsey. She loves shopping. She basks in the attention of the sales staff and paws over different fabrics and textures. Over the hours, she's tried on new boots and hats, gotten a free makeover and yet she still wasn't finished. To the spa for a manicure was her next stop.

"You're going to wear that hat one time and it'll never be worn again. I don't know why you spend your money on that stuff. I'm starting to believe you are really a shop-a-holic," Jessica says to Chelsey on their way into the nail bar.

"I'm not a shop-a-holic, I can go without. Real shop-a-holics cannot," Chelsey jokes.

"Girl it's an obligation to you. You would rather eat porridge for a whole month so you can have more money to shop than eat a proper diet."

"Can I help you ladies?" the nail technician interrupts the ladies' giggle to ask.

"Yes, two mani and pedi's please," Chelsey answers.

"Okay right this way." Both Jessica and Chelsey follow the tiny Asian to their seat.

"So, what do want Chelsey, because I'm no fool. All this buttering me up stuff comes with a price." Chelsey burst into laughter; her sister knew her too well.

"Just shut-up and let me get you relaxed first," Chelsey jokes.

"Oh, I'm not complaining. I'm about to enjoy all of this." Jessica leans back into the plush leather massage chair and props her feet up.

"So spill the beans chic, what's going on?"

"If I tell you, you promise you won't judge me?" Chelsey's tone drops from enthusiasm to pitiful.

"Oh shit, this sounds heavy. What has David done now?"

Quickly Chelsey snaps, "Why it got to be something about David?"

"I don't know who you be thinking you're fooling, but I know you more than you know yourself Chelsey and the only time you start a conversation off like this is when it's about David. So, again ask you, what has David done now?" Chelsey toys around with the temperature of the blue-lit water that's filling up in the bowl. She's too embarrassed to look up and face Jessica.

"Ma'am is it too hot for you?" the nail tech asks.

"No, it's nothing wrong with the damn water. She's just trying avoid eye contact," Jessica snaps.

"He's done nothing, all right. I just miss him, that's all." Jessica knew she would eventually push Chelsey hard enough to explode.

"To be quite honest with you, I never stop missing him."

"That's no surprise," Jessica replies.

"Seeing him again brought back these feelings I had hidden deep inside. Love, lust and passion. No man could fill that void."

"Wait a damn minute! When did you sneak off to New York?" Jessica blurts.

"I didn't, he's Chloe's new professor."

"So you mean to tell me this nigga…" the black guest and Asian techs eyes fixates on Jessica. The word nigga coming from a white woman's mouth was never acceptable.

"Will you watch your mouth and lower your tone? Damn!"

"Oh, that's my bad. But you mean to tell this nigga is Chloe's professor? What happened to him not wanting to bother yaw and all that mess?"

"He said he didn't know about Chloe attending the school and he would leave if he had another job lined up but he doesn't."

Nodding her head, Jessica replies, "Well I understand that but… So, what are you going to do Chelsey?"

"I don't know. I put love from my mind discarding it as though it was nothing more than a pair of shoes that I've outgrown a long time ago Jessica." Speechless, Jessica just listens. She can tell Chelsey needs an ear, not a judge.

"There is an ache that comes and goes, always returning in quiet moments. I want so much to be back close to him, to talk and laugh like we once did. But I know that nothing good can come of it right now or ever. But then I feel like I'd rather take the pain than to go without his love at all. You know?"

"Yeah, I hear you sister. I do know love isn't something you can just turn off."

"I keep thinking maybe in a few years we can be together again, close, happy... Then we can have something that is actually good, love that has a chance of lasting."

"You probably don't have to wait that long Chelsey. I mean the girls are grown now. I don't see why you and him can't try and rekindle old flames." Surprised at Jessica's response, Chelsey turns her body to face Jessica.

"Did I just hear what I thought I heard?"

"Yeah, I mean why not? By sides his little problem, he really is a good man and since..." Jessica checks the scenery to see if anyone is listening in on their conversation and then continues when she concludes the coast is clear to talk.

"Since the kids are grown, why not?"

"You don't know how much that means to me to hear that from you Jessica. I needed to hear that. For so long I felt like no one understood where I was coming from when I said I couldn't just let him go. I see him everywhere I go - in the things we both love - in nature, in music, in silly things we once laughed at. Though he's been gone, his aura remains with me, making the pain all the worse, keeping the feelings so raw."

"I'll say this and leave it alone. Girl go get your man! The kids are grown and doing them now but don't bring him to the house until

Clover is out away to college." Chelsey's day has gone better than she could have planned it. She leaves the mall feeling hopeful of a brighter future. A future where she is happily in love again.

CHAPTER 27

"**B**eside the errors, mark the comments in red. I want the students to see where they went wrong." Luck has no play in Chloe snagging the new student assistant job but every day she feels like a lottery winner. She gets to spend endless time with David, talk to him privately, flirt and even brush up against him on the sly every now and then.

"So how many papers have you done so far?" Chloe is grading papers but as usual her mind begins to wander. One glance into David's captivating bedroom eyes and she gets lost into a fantasy. Undressing him with her eyeballs. She imagines him and her alone in the class as they often were, but instead of just going about the course of a normal day, he has her bent over his desk, fucking her doggy-style from behind. The thought of it makes her pussy wet.

She twirls her kinky-curls with her index finger, biting down on her lips watching David as if he's the only steak in a salad bar.

"Chloe to earth." One flash of his charismatic smile, and Chloe is hypnotized. Her eyes follow him around the room. *This man can get my pussy wet by his looks alone. Look at his body, dayum, how did I get so lucky?*

He's cut to perfection and it looks like his muscles are chiseled out of stone. Chloe thinks, tapping the pen on the desk, staring blankly into David's dark bedroom eyes.

"Do you want to tell me what's got you so distracted?" Finally, Chloe snaps back into reality.

"I'm sorry, what did you say?"

"What's got you so distracted?" David repeats.

"If I tell you, you promise not to judge?" Chloe answers seductively. She pulls in closer to David's private space. Up until this point, he had kept a very professional relationship with Chloe during school hours. His actions had made the boundaries very clear to her.

"I'm not God, therefor I'm qualified to judge." Her lips brush his. Not innocently, but like a tease, hot, fiery, passionate and demanding. David wants to pull away before he loses himself but he can't seem to. In this very moment, his senses have been seduced and he can no longer think straight.

"Daddy," she whispers slowly, prolonging each letter as if to savor them. He smiles, his heart fluttering at her voice as she clasps her hands on both side of his face.

"Never has my name ever felt so wonderful," he murmurs before she leans in for a big wet one. She kisses him and the outside world is a blur. It was slow and soft, comforting in ways that words would never be. Her hands rest below his ear, her thumb caressing his cheek as their breath mingled. He runs his hands down her spine, pulling her closer until there was no space left between them and he could feel the beating of her heart against his chest. Their tongues wrestle for endless moments before there is a distraction.

"Are you fucking kidding me?" Chelsey's echo bounces off the walls of the classroom. Chloe stays glued to her spot, stiffly moving her hair away from her cheekbones, tucking it behind her ear. She is terrified and so is David. His face is paler than Chloe ever recalled it being. It was as if his very blood was shrinking away from his presence, his lips sealed despite Chelsey's loud outburst.

"Chloe, I'm your mother. How could you be so cold?" Chloe keeps her eyes steady, resting on Chelsey's face. Her moves were unpredictable.

"David, how could you do this to me?" Chelsey's features buckle just slightly before she speaks of the betrayal. Her voice cracking, her pain is more vivid than the guilt on David's face.

"You have no fuckin' heart. I loved you with all of me! There was a time I gladly took torture for you, to protect you, remember? Or do I need to give you details to refresh your memory?" David breaks his gaze. Instead of resting his eyes on Chelsey, he fixates them on the door behind her. He couldn't afford his students walking in on the drama.

"Chelsey, calm down," he peacefully demands.

"Calm down!" she repeats.

"Yes, this is not the place for this." Silently, Chloe watches the two go back and forth.

"Oh, now it's not the place for this? But it's the place for you to make-out with your step-daughter!" Just as "daughter" rolls from Chelsey's tongue, students begin piling in.

"Chelsey, I'm sorry. I love you and I never meant to hurt you. Can we please talk about this later? Please?" he mumbles, attempting to push her out the classroom.

"You love me!" she shouts out. "Yet you gave me up as soon as there was a threat to yourself. That isn't love, or at least not a version of it I can respect. You broke me David, and now you're attacking the only good pieces of me that's left." Slowly, sorrow begins to build up in Chloe. The room is filling up and she knows there is no way to stop the nightmare from happening.

"She's your daughter, David!" So full of rage, Chelsey cannot get a hold of her emotions. "How am I supposed to function after this? Look at what you've done. There isn't a woman alive that wants a man who would betray her like this. At the first sight of temptation, you should have put the gun to your head and pulled the trigger. You'd should have rather died than make-out with your fucking daughter." The small bickering increases, this drama is thicker than any storyline on soap opera. Everyone is shocked of the accusations. Some students stand stale with their hands covering their mouth and others are simply shaking their heads in disgust.

"Oh my God! Your daughter?" one student yells out.

"This is not the place for this Chelsey, please!" Beyond embarrassed, Chloe dashes out the classroom with a handful of tears, but Chelsey pays her or David no mind. She's determined to make her point before being escorted out.

"You know, it's what I would have done if your shoes were on my feet David. Hell, in a way, for you I have pulled the trigger. For years, I've played Russian Roulette with my life for your love. But no more. You will pay for this. I'm done being your bullet proof vest. You need help and I'm going to see to it that you get it." Aggressively, Chelsey jerks away from campus security and then storms out the classroom.

CHAPTER 28

Taking a moment to gather her emotions, Chloe stops in front of her dorm room door. She didn't feel like explaining to Kelly why she was a train wreck, so she wipes the dripping tears from her face and tries her best to get control of her feelings before entering.

Kelly: "Get out before I break your God damn face!"

Chloe: "What?"

Kelly: "Don't push me, Chloe. Get out!" The pain on Kelly face is vivid and Chloe assumes right off back, Kelly attitude is because of Lloyd.

Chloe: "You aren't angry, you're hurt. Or maybe you're angry because you're hurt. Which is it, Kelly?"

Kelly: "Yes, I'm fucking hurt and you know that shit. You knew all the long what was going on. You fucking snake!" Kelly tosses a piece of paper at Chloe's face.

Kelly: "If you were even half as smart as you think you are, you wouldn't still be here."

Chloe: "If you were half as angry as you pretend to be I'd have a black eye and broken ribs already. So, shut up and get a grip. I don't have time for your bullshit. I have my own shit to deal with. You knew that nigga was no good from the start."

"I don't need you verbally pissing all over my feelings today Chloe, and if he is so bad for me, what the hell you think he's going to do to your sister? He's taking her to New York to drag her ass! If you bitches think for a second you're going to live the good life without a price, you're in for a treat. I know the real Lloyd and your little precious sister will too, soon."

"What the fuck are you even talking about Kelly? Like seriously, you're tripping."

"Oh my goodness! Stop acting clueless and just admit the shit already!"

"Admit what?" Chloe snaps.

"Admit that you hooked your sister up with Lloyd behind my back." Chloe bends down to pick up the paper from the floor, hoping to get answers to the chaos and she did.

Hey Chloe, I hope you forgive me for the things I said as I forgive you for the things you said. I just wanted to write you to let you know I'm off to New York with Lloyd. He got drafted, so he had to move and he wanted me to go with him. We're getting married as soon as we settle. Let momma know for me. Talk to you soon.

Signed Clover

Chloe grabs onto the desk chair so that her violent shaking would not cause her to fall. From her eyes come a thicker flow of tears than she had cried for even her own mother as a kid. Her cry is so raw that even Kelly's eyes were suddenly wet with tears. At that moment, Kelly realized Chloe wasn't lying. She knew nothing about anything.

"That bastard took my sister away from me." Chloe cries as if her brain is being shredded from the inside. Emotional pain flows out of her every pore as she struggles between sobs to say, "I'm going to kill that fucker." Kelly can't help herself; she kneels to the floor where Chloe has fallen to comfort her. Her heart no longer aches for her but for Chloe. All night she holds Chloe in her arms, rocking her as if she is a ten-month-old baby. The tears wouldn't stop flowing.

Chloe feels she's lost Clover to Lloyd for good. Life for her went from bad to worse within twenty-four hours.

CHAPTER 29

Five months later

"So, how did going through all of this in front of your classmates make you feel?" Chloe kicks up her feet on the comfy leather sofa and immediately her body relaxes. Her tongue is already asking for a drink of water and the conversation hasn't even picked up yet.

Hesitantly, she responds, "I was mortified. Frozen in my step." She inhales through her mouth; her throat tightens as she remembers the horrific day. The fear is still fresh.

"I couldn't believe it was happening, and in front of everybody too. I stood soaking in the cruel laughter of my classmates; my head was spinning. I've never felt so ashamed in all my life. I knew people would remind me of this every chance they got, so I dropped out of school. There is nothing for me there anymore. Fortunately for me, David knew some literary agents in New York. I left town for a minute, got a book deal and now everything is all good."

Morgan glances at her paperwork, scribbling this or that, then occasionally glances up at Chloe with a question or comment.

"Do you think you can run from the incident forever?" Chloe giggles at the thought.

"Not unless I cast off my identity and start off somewhere new."

"Would you cast of your identity?"

"I don't know, would you Morgan?" Chloe asks.

"I wouldn't but this isn't about me, it's about you Chloe." Morgan's tone never changes, it's one of mellow and calmness.

"I would if David wanted to."

"So are you still with David, Chloe?"

"Yes and it feels good. I'm happier now than I've been my entire life."

"So do you ever get sad or feel bad about your decisions? Do you have any regrets?" Chloe takes a minute to think about the question.

She wants to be respectful; she feels showing remorse would be the decent human thing to do but she has none.

"No, I don't have any regrets. I don't feel bad about anything either. I only felt sad once and that's when I didn't have my sister to share my great news with. I always envisioned us jumping up and down screaming when I got my first book deal but it didn't happen that way." A web of tears builds up in the corners of Chloe's eyes. Morgan deliberately looks out the window to make Chloe feel less shame. She doesn't need Chloe to feel embarrassed and shut down. It's her job to make her feel comfortable enough to be open.

"Have you tried to reach out to your sister?"

"I did once when I was in New York. She refused to see me."

"Did you only try once?" Morgan's jotting increases.

"I assumed Chelsey had spoken with her and she didn't want anything to do with me, so I just left it alone altogether." Now Chloe is looking out the window. The conversation is heating up and Chloe can't bear to face Morgan. For the first time in months, Chloe feel sympathy for herself.

"How about Chelsey?"

"What about her?"

"Have you tried to reach out to her?" Slowly, Chloe sits up on the sofa.

"You see, that's why I'm here doctor."

"Why are you here Chloe?"

"I'm here because I don't know how to handle the Chelsey situation. I love her, I do, but I know I love David more and I know she would never accept us together. So, I don't know if I should just leave well enough alone or if I should try and reach out to Chelsey."

Without a second thought Morgan answers, "I believe you should definitely try and reach out."

"The two of you need to talk, even if it's to get closure. You never know, she may even be willing to patch things up for the sake of growth. You are her child and a mother's love is powerful. I don't believe you'll be able to live with yourself or truly be happy with David until you talk to Chelsey. So, I want you to make that your assignment and the next time you visit, we'll talk about it."

With a pitch in her voice Chloe replies, "Cool." Although she was everything but cool. The mere thought of talking to Chelsey frightens her.

CHAPTER 30

"Hey beautiful, are you here alone?" Chloe's cheeks are suddenly kissed pink like a spring rose, the blooming color is so cute against her freckled skin. She looks away and finds a distraction on the shelf, tossing the canned corn in her basket. David stands back on his leg gawking at Chloe with his bedroom eyes, allowing her time to compose herself, fighting back the smile that wants to break out.

"Did it hurt?"

"What David?" Chloe snaps pushing the cart down the aisle.

"When you fell from heaven." Chloe's blush sears through her cheeks and for a minute she thinks her face is on fire. She suddenly feels awkward, reserved, and coy; even going as far as attempting to hide her rosy features behind her slim fingers.

Chloe's giggles travel down the aisles and Jessica catches hold to it. She peeks her head around the corner and sure enough it was Chloe's voice she heard.

"I know you tired," David continues with his corny jokes. Chloe's laughter was his drug.

"Why would I be tired David?"

"Because you been running through my mind all day." Every time David opens his mouth, Jessica get angrier.

"Baby, did you get the hamburger helper?" At first, Jessica was going to tend to her own business and just go on about her day as if she didn't see David and Chloe, but the thought of keeping silent made her blood boil even more and out of the blue she just snaps.

"You two muthafuckas are sick!" Jessica's rage came out faster than magma and was just as destructive. Both David and Chloe turn to face her. Stuck in their steps, the two of them are speechless and could shit fear right onto the floor with just one push.

"How could yawl do her this way? You mean to tell me, you two muthafuckas are actually together?" Jessica's voice travels through the store and slowly shoppers begin to stop and look on.

"My sister loved you both unconditionally. She took your little homeless ass in when you had nowhere to go and gave you a life to be proud of and this is how you repay her?" Chloe shrivels before Jessica, but she keeps on going, stopping short of physical violence, but doing far more damage with her words.

"And you David!" Scared of what Jessica might say, David takes Chloe's hand and leads her out the grocery store, but sure enough, Jessica follows close behind.

"You ought to be thanking my sister your ass is not in jail instead of repaying with betrayal. She could have let your ass hang out to dry." David speeds up his pace, but he couldn't make it to the car fast enough.

"I haven't heard from my sister in weeks. She won't even answer her phone she's so hurt." Finally, David and Chloe reach the Jeep. Rapidly, they jump into the jeep and snap on their seat belts. The quicker they can ditch the scene the better. Jessica is crying in the middle of parking lot and the attention they're getting is embarrassing.

"You can at least call her Chloe! She needs to hear from you. Her heart is broken." Jessica sobs out as the Jeep pulls off. The ride home is a silent and awkward one and to make matters worse, Chloe couldn't get Jessica's words out of her head.

"You can at least call her Chloe! She needs to hear from you. Her heart is broken."

Daring herself not to cry, Chloe didn't blink much on the way home. It just wasn't the time for weakness but for the first time since being with David, Chloe's heart wants to cry for Chelsey. She just couldn't tell him that. She couldn't make him feel like the villain.

CHAPTER 31

Weeks have passed since David and Chloe's run in with Jessica and finally, Chloe can sleep again. She hasn't dreamed about Chelsey in two days. The haunting dreams had her waking up before David, and now she doesn't even hear him leaving for work. If it wasn't for her annoying alarm clock, she would probably sleep the day away.

"Alright, alright, alright!" she yells at the clock as she brings her hand down in a semi-drunken floppiness to hit the alarm clock. Slowly and reluctantly, Chloe uncovers her face. Blink, close her eyes, and blink again. Streaks of sunlight penetrate the window and blind her. She sits up, drags her feet off the bed, and rub her knuckles onto her eyes. She has a full day ahead and all she wants to do is sleep. Her very first signing in Atlanta is today and there are so many things that need to be done.

She stretches her arms above her head and yawns. *I need to stop by the shop and get my eyebrows done, call Taylor and make sure she has the book ends, bookmarks, pens, table cloth and raffle tickets.* She reflects as she watches her legs dangle above the off-white polyester carpet. *Oh, yeah, I need to call the restaurant and make sure the reservations are squared away.* She thinks right before she jumps up from the bed.

"Okay, get up Chloe. Pull it together." Before Chloe can reach the bathroom, she's stopped in tracks by her ringing phone.

"That's probably Taylor right there," she assumes.

"Hey Taylor," the awkward silence on the phone makes Chloe look at her caller I.D.

"Hello, who is this?" Instantly her gut tells her the private number is Chelsey and she contemplates on hanging up.

"Did you ever call Chelsey?" It's a relief to know that the Jane Doe is Jessica and not Chelsey, but Chloe didn't want to speak to Jessica either, so she snaps.

"Look Jessica, I don't have time for this today. I have too much on my plate. I'll have to call you call back."

"Chelsey is dead!" Jessica blurts before Chloe hangs up.

"What? What kind of games are you playing lady!" Pissed, Chloe begins pacing the floor. Her blood is boiling.

"I don't have time for this and it's very sick of you to go through all this just to get attention. I mean, who would play like that? You're more concerned about me and Chelsey talking than she is. I don't have time for this stupid stuff!" Chloe's echo travels throughout the house.

"I asked if you had to talked to her because I was hoping you did before she killed herself. But from your response, I can tell that you haven't. This isn't a joke Chloe. They found my sister dead from an overdose of pills." Chloe bites down on her lower lip and her eyes turn glossy with tears. She tries to blink them away and when she realizes that she can't, she flops back onto the bed.

"Chloe are you there?" Jessica shrieks through the phone.

"Yes, I'm here. I'll have to call you back."

"No, wait. Listen, I need you…." *Click….* Like a miracle on Christmas day David appears through the door with the perfect mix of Tulips and Iris freshly cut flowers, ready to impress.

He heard Chloe yelling from downstairs and immediately he rushes to her rescue. He assumes she's stressing over the book signing and wants to inform her that he took the day off to be her do-boy.

"No need to stress, your Do-Boy is here," he sings. Chloe hides her tears, and with it all the pain she's feeling. And when she looks up at David she turns into a different person. She manages to fake a smile that buries her pain deep inside her heart. But her eyes remain cold, like nothing in this world could melt them.

"I thought you were gone to work?" she manages to say.

"Nope, I was out getting you breakfast and flowers. I took the day off so I can be here for you physically and emotionally." David's charismatic smile could usually light up a room but it wasn't working today. The room was as dark as a cave, even with the sun beaming through the blinds.

"I know how stressful book signings can be and I don't want you to stress. I just want you to enjoy the beauty of your accomplishment today. So, what can I help you with first?"

There was no right way to bring the news to David, so Chloe just blurts it, "Chelsey overdosed on pills." David's face falls faster than a corpse in cement boots.

In this instant, his skin becomes gray, his mouth hangs with lips slightly parted and his eyes are as wide as they can stretch. *Shit, I probably should have told him better than that,* Chloe thinks.

"Don't you worry about anything. I'll see what's going on. Don't you worry about anything," he responds wrapping her tightly in his arms.

"David are you alright?" Chloe knew the answer to the question but she desperately wants to hear David say, *no* but he doesn't. Instead, he hides his emotions beneath the surface of his hardened facial expression.

"Yes, I'm okay Chloe. Don't you worry about me and don't you worry about the book signing either. I'll take care of everything. I'll get it rescheduled. I'll go talk to Jessica too. You just lay down and try to get some sleep and if you are up to it, try and call your sister later." David transitions into full daddy mode and like an obedient child, Chloe obeys. She dives back into bed hoping to block out the pain from reality.

"Are you sure you're fine?" Chloe asks right before David exits the room.

"Yes Chloe, I'll be fine. You just get some rest and let me go figure things out. I'll talk to you when you wake."

"Okay," she replies before tucking herself deep under the thick, quilted blanket.

CHAPTER 32

The funeral is all black clothes and white waxy faces, every one of them with puffy red eyes. If looks could kill, both Chloe and David would be dead. They can feel the angry eyes burning through their skin as they nervously walk up to the casket to view Chelsey's body.

"Nooooo!" Chloe cries out before falling short to her knees. Seeing Chelsey in a casket is too much for her to bear and she loses the little cool she had. After a little work, the pallbearers and David finally get Chloe to her seat, and no more than five minutes later, it's time for her to get right back up to share her best memories of Chelsey. David had insisted that she didn't, but she's determined to show her respect. It's funeral etiquette for family and friends to share their best memories, and since Clover is a no show, Chelsey feels it's the least she can do.

Grief tares at her insides like a tornado, as she climbs the three steps to the podium, before she can even stand up straight tears fall thickly and her voice becomes stuck in her throat. She waves off the pallbearers and David and finally utters her first words.

"The saying goes, *you never know how much you love a person until you don't have them to love anymore.* It's no secret, I haven't been the best daughter." The crying in the church increases as Chloe takes her time to get her words out.

"I haven't been the best daughter but Chelsey has always been the best mother. I have a lot of regrets but my biggest one is not talking to you before God called you home. Chelsey, if you are hearing me right now. Please forgive me for the wrong I have done. I love you momma and I'm praying that you are resting in peace now." Chloe breaks into extreme sobbing. She can barely breathe. Close friends and family members instantly provide sympathy on demand.

At this very moment, no one is worried about Chloe's past decisions but her health. The sight is too much for David and finally, he breaks his calm demeanor and breaks down. But not one soul takes notice, except Chloe. His crying is what picks her back up. By the time she gets down from the podium, David is gone and Chloe is stuck in Jessica's arms impatiently waiting for the service to be over.

The funeral service seems to be going slower than a roast cooking in a crockpot. Everyone has a memory to share, a favorite hymn to sing. Jessica must have agreed to every request. Half way through the service and the old ladies are swaying on their feet. If it wasn't for the cool wind pushing through the open church doors, there might have been more to bury than just Chelsey.

****

Chloe barges into the house with rage. She's pissed for many reasons, one being David leaving her to deal with the wolves by herself. As soon as her eyes locks on David she charges him. David backs into the wall. Chloe is unrecognizable; red in the face with her limbs swinging left to right in violent chaotic strikes. Likely half the neighborhood could hear her screaming.

"You bastard!" Without second thought, David assumes Jessica has spoken to Chloe about his ill past. So, he just folds up like a coward and allows Chloe to take her frustration out on his forearms, chest and head. That's until Chloe blurts out, "Why didn't you tell me you still loved her? Why didn't you tell me? I would have let yawl be." Relief, that his assumption was wrong, David pushes himself out the corner and quickly grabs hold of Chloe from behind. His arms restrain her like a white jacket.

"Chloe, listen to me. Stop. Listen! I will always have love for Chelsey. I just wasn't in love with her." Like a baby, Chloe breaks back into tears, only this time she doesn't fall. David holds her tight in his arms. The two eat the food Chloe packed from reception at Jessica's house kicked up in front of the television watching Chelsey's favorite show, *I Love Lucy*. Chloe notices that David is asleep and decides to slip from underneath his bear hug. Quietly she writes him a note and then sneaks out the door.

David, I need some space, so I'm checking into a room tonight. I hope you understand. Don't worry about me either, I'll be fine. I just need a little air. I will call you soon.

Signed Chloe

CHAPTER 33

Slowly, Chloe approaches the big tree in Chelsey's yard; a gentle smile graces her lips. The cool wind is like a music of old memories to her. She touches the tree, tracing old drawings that she and Clover did on that very tree long ago. *Those were the good ole days;* she reflects as there was nothing for her and Clover to stress or worry about back then. Chelsey, did all the worrying and in private. So, the girls would have no clue.

The leaves sweep over the ground and take small flights into the air. *Don't be out there playing in the leaf piles.* Chloe tosses her head back and raises her eyes to the sky. She could hear Chelsey just screaming out at her. A smile spreads from freckled cheek to cheek. Her mind relaxes a little, and for a short moment she feels the happiness of her childhood life bubble up from within. But the joy isn't strong enough to fight the pain.

If it wasn't for the passing cars she would fall out like a little girl not getting her way, arms out wide and legs kicking, but instead she keeps her hands in her pockets and inhales deeply before entering the house. Nothing feels the same. The house just didn't feel like a home without Chelsey there.

For the first time, Chloe didn't smell perfume, chicken frying, or holiday candles burning when she enters. There is no Beetles or Michael music playing. It was as if the spirit of the house had gone with Chelsey. The little house had never looked so dusty and that simple thought frightens her because now it is her job to bring those feelings back to life. Chelsey left her and Clover the house but everything is in Chloe's control. Which she couldn't understand, why.

She flops onto the couch and finally pops open the letter Chelsey left behind for her. She knew it was going to be deep, so she wanted to be alone when she read it.

Hello Chloe, it's your momma Chelsey. Yes, I'm still your mother. ☺ Where should I start? I guess by stating that I love you and I always will. You and your sister were the best thing to ever happen to me and I don't regret taking you in, not one bit. You girls were my life and I couldn't imagine my life without yawl.

In fact, the reason you're reading this letter is probably because I felt like I lost you girls and I just couldn't live my life without my babies. But don't worry about me, I'm in a better place now and I don't want you two to feel guilty about anything either. I forgive yaw and it's not your fault. I shouldn't have sheltered yaw from the real world. David took advantage of your vulnerability and that's my fault. As a mother, I should have never had yawl around a pedophile.

This letter is on two cent paper, but the words are without price. Everything Chelsey says is horror music to Chloe; every word stings, and the approaching topic has Chloe's blood boiling. Her palms are sweaty and her nerves are on edge like when she watches scary movies with Clover. She pictures Chelsey writing the letter drinking her favorite wine with tears flowing from her eyes like a running fountain. The words flowing from her mind to her heart, down her arm to the pen and the paper. *This must have been hard to do*; Chloe thinks before quickly folding the letter back into her pockets. The roaring engine pulling into the driveway startles her and she assumes that David has come for her.

She wipes her tears and tries to paste on a smile as she runs to the door. The plan is to brush him off. She can't afford to talk to him right now. She would probably slip and tell him about the letter and he would probably freak out or be pissed if he read the letter. The topic was getting too deep.

"Chloe," the soft voice is low and Chloe doesn't recognize it at first but on the second shriek, "Chloe!" she catches a clue.

"Clover!" she yells back.

"Yes!" When Clover first comes into view, Chloe doesn't recognize her, she's too far away and her gait is all wrong. She walks like a scarecrow more than a lady and all lop-sided at that. As she nears, Chloe's heart falls right through her sneakers. Clover's more purple than brown. Her left eye is swollen; she can't be seeing a thing out of that and she won't for a while.

Her face bears frozen blood and her clothes are an utter mess. Then she tries to say Chloe's name, "Chloe." Her cracked lips failing at the first syllable, but she doesn't need to call Chloe anymore, she's already running to her in full speed.

"Clover sister, are you okay?" Clover grabs onto her full belly, gently rubs it and answers, "I am now. Now that I see you." For endless moments, the two hug one another tightly, rocking side-to-side in the driveway.

"Come on, come inside," Chloe mumbles before leading the way.

"I'm sorry I missed the funeral. I had to fight my way here." Clover giggles at her own joke but nothing was funny. She had been living in heaven and hell with Lloyd. Things were either really good or really bad.

"What happened, are you okay?" Concern shrieks from Chloe's tone but Clover just ignores it and changes the subject.

"How was the funeral?" Taking notice to Clover's chess move, Chloe goes along with the game. She didn't need her sister getting mad and running off again, so she decides to mind her business.

"It was the saddest thing I've ever seen. You better thank God you weren't there. The drama was real and you know, I was the centerpiece."

"Aww Chloe, don't beat yourself up. Chelsey knows you didn't mean her no harm." Gently, Clover caresses Chloe's kinky curls.

"Did you talk to her?" Chloe asks.

"A couple of times, but I stopped answering the phone for her because she would always ask when I was coming home and I didn't have an answer for her because……" Clover's tone weakens and she quickly murmurs the last of her sentence, "Well because Lloyd gets very busy and we hadn't had time to put a visit in our schedule."

"I understand," Chloe responds while pulling the letter back out her pocket.

"Well she left us a note. I was just reading it before you arrived. I guess we can read it together." Without warning, tears pour from Clover's swollen eyes.

"Aww, don't cry Clover. I can't take seeing you cry. We'll get through this, together."

"I'm fine," Clover sobs.

"Let's just read the letter."

"Okay, I'll start from the beginning."

Hello Chloe, it's your momma Chelsey. Yes, I'm still your mother. ☺ Where should I start? I guess by stating that I love you and I always will. You and your sister were the best thing to ever happen to me and I don't regret taking you in, not one bit. You girls were my life and I couldn't imagine my life without yawl.

In fact, the reason you're reading this letter is probably because I felt like I lost you girls and I just couldn't live my life without my babies. But don't worry about me, I'm in a better place now and I don't want you two to feel guilty about anything either. I forgive yaw both and it's not your fault. I shouldn't have sheltered yaw from the real world. Chloe, David took advantage of your vulnerability and that's my fault. As a mother, I should have never had yawl around a pedophile. He's had his eyes on you since you were a kid and I didn't protect you like I should have but I did put him out our house and I thought I had erased him out of our lives but I didn't and for that, Chloe I'm sorry.

Clover, I should have told you more about your biological mother and maybe you would have tried harder not to repeat her mistakes. Baby girl you must break the cycle. Your mother was a victim of domestic violence. That's how she died. Your father killed her. I *pray you get the strength you need to break free of the chain.*

I write this letter to you girls in hope that it helps change your bad habits and to let you know that I love you and always will. The house is yawl's, Chloe, you're in charge of course. Have me some grand babies and dress the house with their pictures. Remember your mother Chelsey, love you girls always.

Both Clover and Chloe's sobbing increases. It was like Chelsey was still mothering them, even from her grave. Jessica could hear the sobbing as she approaches the house, and without knocking she barges right on in. She didn't need to ask why they were crying. It was obvious that they had read the letter. She read the letter before giving it to Chloe and she knew it would rip their hearts to shreds. With no invite, she flops onto the sofa with the girls and wrap them both up in her arms.

"I love you girls and you will always have me," she mumbles to them.

"Thank you aunt," Clover replies between sniffles.

"Excuse me for a minute." Chloe jumps up from the sofa and pulls her phone from her pocket. After three rings, David answers.

"Hey beautiful, are you okay? Did you make it to the room?"

"I guess I just made it easy for you to get what you always wanted. You are a sick bastard! How could you David?" David was sure this time, Chloe was in on his past.

Both Jessica and Clover watch in silence as Chloe yells her frustration through the phone.

"I trusted you! Chelsey trusted you……"

"I'm sorry Chloe. Have a nice life," David interrupts Chloe to say before ending the phone call. Stunned, she looks at the phone for assurance, and sure enough the phone call had ended.

"He hung up on me, that bastard!" Jessica rushes to Chloe's rescue before she can fall short to her knees.

"Baby, don't let him win. Forgive him and just be thankful you know the truth and that part of your life is behind you." Clover attempts to join the hurdle on the floor and in unison Jessica and Chloe shout, "Noooo, you shouldn't be on your knees!"

Clover snickers and replies, "Dang, okay." Together the ladies laugh.

"I'm going to be an aunt; I'm going to be an aunt," Chloe sings and just like that the mood had changed.

"Let's make a vow to never leave each other's side again," Chloe blurts out the blue.

"Cool," Jessica responds instantly.

"Clover, you don't have to worry about anything. I will help you raise the baby. You don't have to go back to Lloyd. I got you."

"So do I," Jessica adds to Chloe's comment. But Clover is silent. Both Jessica and Chloe look at each other worried, but they ignore Clover's silence and Jessica changes the subject.

"Let's look at some of these pictures." Jessica snatches the photo album off the coffee table and for the rest of the night the girls look at pictures, remember, Chelsey and giggle their hearts away.

The End

Maybe ☺

Made in the USA
Las Vegas, NV
03 February 2022